THE
JANUARY
GIRL

THE JANUARY GIRL

A Novel

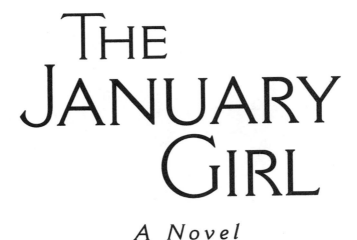

Goldie Taylor

NEW YORK

A Black Expressions® book published by Madison Park Press, 15 East 26th Street, New York, NY 10010. Madison Park Press is a trademark of Bookspan.

Book design by Christos Peterson

ISBN: 978-1-58288-253-6

Printed in the United States of America

TO CORNELIUS
For the many ways you continue to bless me

IN MEMORIUM
Wyart Taylor, Jr. (1943–1973)
Christopher John Byndon Taylor (1968–1991)
Don Edwin Hughes (1959–2005)

ACKNOWLEDGMENTS

"Trouble don't last always," Miss Alice used to say. "Joy," she said, "comes in the morning."

Alice Robinson Cole was my maternal grandmother, the one who took me over her knee when I committed one misdeed or another, and made me laugh as she checkered Bible verses with expletives. She was the one who bathed my little brown behind in Ivory soap until it was clean, and the one who slathered my chest with Vicks VapoRub when I was sick from eating snow. As I put the final draft of this work to bed on New Year's Eve of 2005, I turned to her picture, perched on the top shelf of my bookcase, and thought back on all of the wonderful lessons she'd imparted. She taught me to say "thank you" and to appreciate the blessings and mercies of God, to watch the miracles unfold. In my life, I have been incredibly blessed with so much and known the goodness of His mercy. I have lived a life replete with miracles.

Over the years, there was a cast of family, friends, and colleagues who kept reminding me that morning was coming. They brought bucket loads of encouragement, pushing me to find and live out my personal truth. I begin with my mentor and friend Don Logan, former Chairman of Time Warner Media & Communications Group. I am especially grateful for your calm, assuring voice when various storms were tearing through my professional life like a straw hut. I owe you a margarita!

I am blessed to have a mother, Mary Alice Taylor, who encouraged me early on, when we were still living in the projects, by buying mail-order books on her meager salary. She couldn't teach me how to bake a perfect sweet potato pie, but she gave me something about living with integrity and honoring my calling. Besides, Auntie Geraldine taught me what to do with a short rib and studied the leaves as I learned to clean turnips over the kitchen sink.

This book might never have been started in the first place without Carol Mackey, Editor-in-Chief of Black Expressions Book Club. I will never ever forget the "henhouse" lunch where this book was born. We laughed about our own foibles, the men who have come and gone, those who stayed far too long, and how we loved them almost in spite of ourselves and even when they proved less than deserving. How even then, when we thought we had nothing else to give anybody new, somehow there was always more. We've been sisters in spirit every single day since. And for the new best friend I've never met, Monica Harris. As I write this, you're in the thick of the editing process. Thank you for helping me make sense.

The characters in this book were inspired, in part, by some of my closest friends. Dr. Millard J. Collier and Honorable Terrell L. Slayton, I am so very grateful that our roads met. To everything there is a season. You were always ready with shoulders to lean on when I turned up rain soaked on your doorsteps. But no shoulders were broader or stronger than those of Elgin Clemons—my lawyer, my friend, a giant among men. It is with reverence and gratitude that I say thank you for all that you've come to mean in a short period of time. You didn't just listen to the words, but you heard the spaces between them.

I deeply appreciate the confidence and support of my literary agent, Larry Kirshbaum. It isn't every day that a little brown girl raised in the dirt and weeds of East St. Louis meets up with a publishing industry legend. Your mother grew up in St. Louis, too? I knew I liked something about you!

To DeBorah Wilson, who read and reread every draft. You are my very own personal angel. Because of you, I kept fighting to write, to love, and to live. There are others to thank, including Hal Logan and Etienne LeGrand (thanks for lending me your name), Mark and Darlene Trigg, Larry and Linda Hart Johnson, "Professor" John Simley, Dr. Will McDade, Howard Spiller, Rich Coleman, Reuben McDaniel III, Scott Sillers, Larry Norvell, Lisa May Evans, Sheryll Campbell, Clay Merrill, Sylvester Monroe, and my sister-girl Vicki Brown. If I thanked you each a thousand times a piece, a thousand times a day, for a thousand years, it would never be enough.

For my three incredible teenagers: Katherine, Joshua, and Haley. Thank you for lighting my path. Of all that I am, I am most proud to be your mother. Even if, from time to time, you are proof positive indeed that God has a sense of humor.

And finally . . . for Cornelius, to whom this book is dedicated. When you look at me, I feel like the sum total of every woman in the world, capable of anything, truly worthy of everything. A girl should be so lucky. I cannot begin to count up the ways you have blessed me; they number the stars. You are my partner, my best friend, my confidante, a gale force wind at my back, my island in rough seas. "Swim pimp, swim!"

"Give your love, live your life, each and every day.
And keep your hands wide open, and let the sun shine through,
'cause you can never lose a thing if it belongs to you."
—Abbey Lincoln

Chapter 1

She didn't seem to notice him leave her side. He slipped out of bed, leaving a sudden emptiness in the tufted, satin-stenciled duvet, a trail of his warmth. It was just after 5:00 a.m., the second Monday in July. The sun would be along soon to burn away the haze and what remained of the cool night's rains.

He showered first, then dressed in a smartly cut suit. A tailor sewn, light linen with subtle striping was his choosing. The soft gray was set off with powder blue lines and a matching breast scarf. He is, and always has been, a man of exteriors. A man unafraid to tell the world that his best was better than theirs. And it is, by almost any measure. He had been born to it, mostly, having inherited his father's wealth and intellect. His own pursuits multiplied those fortunes exponentially. With his mother's good sense, he'd keep it—safe from the eager fingers of a wife he couldn't bring himself to love for more than a day at a time, squired away and waiting for the day of liberation already long overdue.

The home he shares with his wife, Etienne, is an expansive, Mediterranean-styled compound comprised of several buildings, including a small stucco and stone cottage situated on the westerly edge of the lot. Larger and wider than the others along Habersham Drive, the tree-lined main avenue connecting Peachtree Battle with Tuxedo Park, the house is of a size and design that pleases Jack. Situated in one of the most exclusive enclaves in Atlanta, the Gabrielle estate sits just three blocks from the Georgia Governor's Mansion, a stone's throw from downtown but clearly a million miles away. He reveled in the notion that his lily-white neighbors might harbor some jealousy. So what if they resented him? The source of his money was certainly no mystery.

His father had been a physician long before little black boys could ever dream of getting into more than a handful of medical schools. The late Dr. Leland DuBose Gabrielle was a surgeon, one of the best the country had ever known in his time, colored or otherwise.

At his mother's urging, young Jackson followed his father into medicine. There was, in fact, a prescribed recipe, an ordered road set down by his mother, Naomi, an appointed season of harvest, and she would not rest until his feet were firmly planted on the path. His father's wishes and his future were codified in Leland's last will and testament: *Achieve more, get more money.* Jack would not disappoint. But his father had died too soon, when Jack was just fifteen, just three days after his graduation from the ultraexclusive Westminster Academy.

If nothing else, Leland left Jack with the art of dressing well, he thought to himself, as he stood in the dressing room snapping on a pair of pewter cuff links and knotting his vintage silk necktie. Both had belonged to his father. His custom-built closets teamed with fine tailored suits, silk ties, and Italian leather shoes. At forty-three, Jack was now, undoubtedly and without question, a man of appearances and the world was his stage.

As he adjusted the knot in perfect alignment with his neck in front of a bronze-framed mirror, he looked at the reflection and saw his wife's outstretched arms. Etienne's perfectly manicured fingers reached gracefully in the shadowy bedroom, begging him back. He ignored the opportunity to embrace her immediately, but then gave in with just enough emphasis to let her know that he remained her husband, that his commitment to their waning marriage remained. Although he could not see her face clearly, he knew that it was still beautiful, still a wonderfully flawless visage even at this hour.

She wanted more, though he could not give it, nor did he want to. He didn't need her anymore, nor did he need to say it. Still, he let her wrap her arms around his neck. It was the sort of embrace that said she could forgive everything—that after fifteen years, it was worth another try.

"I've got to get to the hospital," he whispered in his signature, sugar-dipped woodsy drawl. "Morning rounds."

"What about lunch?"

There was no leaning timbre in her voice, not a hint of the southern lilt Jack was so fond of using to get his way. Whenever he opened his mouth, the seas began to part; mighty rivers ran in reverse as he sung his words as if quoting Walt Whitman, his charms unnerving for the unwashed masses. Etienne, on the other hand, had been born in France, the daughter of a high-ranking African bishop and a French-Scot woman who was a lay worker in the church. She spent her formative years steeped in affluence and the right society ties of Georgetown. Even after fifteen years of living south of the Mason-Dixon, she still rolled her R's as if it were only yesterday that she had stepped off the train at Brookwood Station.

"Sorry, I've got a speech at the medical school for a group of know-it-all, short-jacketed first year residents."

"Dinner?"

"Medical Association board meeting."

Etienne sighed.

"I'm sorry. I really must . . . I'm sorry."

"Don't say you're sorry. Just stay home," she whispered. "Just today."

"I gotta get to it," he said pulling away.

There had been love, or at least a mutual admiration, in the beginning. At the time, he was in his first year of medical training at Morehouse and she was an undergraduate studying philosophy at neighboring Spelman College. Whatever brought them together then was gone now, he thought with some regret, rank and sour like spoiled milk.

He first plotted his escape when Jack Jr., the first of their boys, was still a toddler, ambling about in his lace-up Buster Browns, attending some insanely expensive day school reserved for the children of the well-heeled and uncommonly rich. Little Jack was among the first handful of black children to attend Westerly Country Day, no small thanks to his father's generous gift to the school's scholarship fund. At the time, Etienne proudly announced his acceptance to her bridge club partners and anyone else within earshot. Good money could still buy favor.

Six years ago Jack got as far as his attorney's office. But like a train running on time, Etienne told him she was pregnant again. A divorce, though long overdue, would have to wait. The waiting turned to a meager brand of complacency, checkered with Saturday morning Little League baseball, Cub Scout meetings, and Wednesday night family movies.

After her father died, he put it off another year. One year became another, then another. While many of his colleagues were blissfully married to second and third wives, having parted with a substantial portion of their fortunes to pave their way to peace, Jack dulled himself with a near constant work schedule and Friday night stops at the Ritz-Carlton. Mr. Elijah, his favorite bartender, reserved a corner table in the rear of the main bar. As usual, he delivered a double shot of top-shelf cognac, a glass of water, and a lime wedge. With every sip, he repeated the math in his head. Divorce was a costly affair, and for Jack that would mean millions, but more than that it would be an admission of failure, something Jack had never known. *How much is too much?*

He conducted the morning rounds on the ward, then went to his office. He spent much of the day thinking about Thandy and the long weekends he used to have with her—days when they would drive five hours south to his summerhouse on Sea Island, an exclusive retreat where old money frolicked in the sun. The private beaches were reserved for those lucky enough to own homes or able to afford a night's stay at The Cloisters. Inherited from his parents, the Lion's Gate estate stood triumphantly on the Black Banks River, just south of Pelican Point where they watched the terns swoop and sway under the purple-ribboned sky. She'd cook him a low-country breakfast of shrimp and grits or an omelet stuffed fat with crabmeat, shrimp, scallions, and peppers. He could watch her water-ski from the private dock, then delight in her worldly ramblings until the sun came up. He marveled in every square inch of her drawn-butter skin, the depth of her caramel eyes speckled with bits of green that lit up when the sun hit them.

Jack paced his office, staving off the cold emptiness, missing the warmth of the girlish laughter he hadn't heard in over a week.

Thandywaye Malone was an exquisitely beautiful creature, steeped in grace, a sheer force of nature. He had dialed her cell three or more times a day, until it was disconnected. The house phone had been cut off, too. It was as if she simply evaporated into the wind.

Chapter 2

Jack stood for a moment in his antique-filled, oak-paneled offices overlooking the Atlanta skyline from "Pill Hill." From his perch, high above a collection of the South's most notable hospitals, clinics, and medical offices, he could see the full northerly perimeter of the city. On a clear day, Kennesaw Mountain appeared to the north and Stone Mountain to the east. It was the domain of someone who has long since arrived.

He admired his newly browned hands. The searing redness had given way to a warm afterglow. The island sun had been good to him. However, the rich, warm tan had been costly, he lamented; his trip to Barbados was uncharacteristically imprudent. He had been back mere hours before the proverbial shit hit the fan. Etienne had been and remained coy about the matter, but the confrontation with Thandy came like a lightning bolt on an otherwise clear and sunny day. After ten years, she simply walked away. She had been his "best girl," the one who preferred his heart to his wallet.

"Dr. Gabrielle," a voice interrupted. "Mrs. Chapman's chart is ready."

His eyes drifted over the horizon, traced the treetops, and floated through the sparse clouds. The interstate below was choked with midday traffic. Jack stared back at his hands, admiring the temporarily bronzed complexion, spreading out the fingers, examining the creases between the tan and paleness. They were gifted hands, wealthy hands, hands that had not known a moment's labor. Everything had been his for the asking. Even Thandy.

"Dr. Gabrielle?" the voice gently demanded. "We're an hour or better behind schedule. If you could just review the blood studies . . ."

Sandy stood impatiently in the door frame, cupping the patient file to her breast. Sandy worried for him. The long hours with no lunch, back-to-back surgeries and an endless string of weekends on call would surely ring defeat for a man half his age, but the office always ran like clockwork. But today was obviously different.

He was always able to work his way through any disappointment the world tried to throw at him, but Thandy refused to be worked. The weight of her absence was surprising even to him.

"Maybe you should take another vacation," Sandy smiled. Twenty years his senior, Sandy worried after Jack as if he were her own son. Often she packed a second sack lunch just in case she could persuade him to eat.

"I think I've had enough sun." Jack sighed and gave her a weak smile.

He took the thick folder, leaned against the corner of his desk, and skimmed through the laboratory reports. He already knew the story, having written most of it himself.

Three years ago, Sonja Chapman first visited her family physician complaining of searing headaches, nausea, and exhaustion. Some days, the young mother was so weak she could not stand. Rest and over-the-counter pain relievers were prescribed, but the symptoms continued. A ration of Phenergan was ordered to manage the nausea. Still, she pleaded for answers. For months, Unison Healthcare turned down the primary physician's referral to see a specialist until she was found unconscious in her bathroom after suffering a grand mal seizure. She was rushed by ambulance to Duke University Medical Center in Durham, North Carolina. The tumor was by then the size of a golf ball and located close to the motor strip. A team of oncologists ruled the demon inoperable and likely malignant. Its location excluded a pre-op biopsy. Even the most gifted surgeon could damage the motor strip and leave her fully paralyzed. Depending on the level of aggression, they advised, Sonja would have four months to live. Fred Chapman, a broad brick of a man who drove a dump truck on double shifts for Carolina Mulch & Erosion Solutions, cradled his wife in his arms and wept. The young couple prayed.

Their answer was Dr. Jackson Gabrielle, a celebrated neurological surgeon practicing five hours south in Atlanta. The following evening, Sonja and Fred arrived by helicopter and checked into Northside Hospital. Sandy was there to greet the gurney on the landing pad. Jack took one look at Sonja's medical history, scrubbed, and went right to work.

He'd closed his eyes and felt her bare skull with the tips of his fingers. He'd marked a spot with a purple marker, then kept feeling, working his way around her head. He'd feel, then mark, then feel, and mark again. The surgical assistant had prepared a table of tools including drills, bone cement, various scalpels, and sutures. A nurse had scrubbed Sonja's head with a foamy antiseptic.

Jack performed an awake-craniotomy using a brain mapping technique pioneered by his father, Dr. Leland Gabrielle. The procedure allowed Jack to talk to Sonja while he operated. As he opened her skull, she guided him away from critical tissue. Once inside, the biopsy revealed that it was an aggressive grade four glioblastoma, multiforme tumor, a devastating sight even for trained eyes. Once he was certain he could excavate the mass, he nodded to Sandy, who opened the stereo cabinet and turned up the volume. Prince's hard metal guitar screeched from the speakers. The louder, the better. The thick bass line lulled him into a comfort zone. His hands steadied and he went to work.

"I never meant 2 cause u any sorrow . . . I never meant 2 cause u any pain."

As the music blared, Jack focused his attention on the tumor. The bleeding stepped up. He steadied himself. Hemostatic clips were used to stop it.

"*U say u want a leader . . . But u can't seem 2 make up your mind. I think u better come . . . And let me guide u . . . 2 the purple rain.*"

As the music segued to Jay-Z's hard rhythms, he reached inside and withdrew the fleshy mass. The surgical nurse placed it in a bowl of sterile saline. Another rushed it off to the lab for a biopsy. Jack examined the impacted section of the brain. Satisfied there was no significant damage, he began closing the incision. When the tissue was secured, he used titanium screws to fasten the skull into position, then began pulling the scalp down. He took a deep breath and sewed it into place.

"*If you're havin' girl problems I feel bad for you son. I got 99 problems but a bitch ain't one!*"

Six hours after they started, Sandy turned off the stereo. Jack emerged from the operating room triumphant and snapped off his latex gloves as if he had conquered all of Mesopotamia. When Jack entered the waiting room, Fred Chapman was already on his feet while the rest of the family remained frozen in their seats. The two men shook hands. Jack got right to the point.

"Mr. Chapman, we believe your wife's tumor was 100 percent resected. We do not expect many physical deficits and those that remain are likely to heal entirely over time. Your wife had a glioblastoma multiforme. We performed a post-operative biopsy to confirm it."

"It is over?"

"Mr. Chapman, your wife is in good shape. She's stable. I cannot say for certain, but I believe we got all of it."

"It is over?" Fred pressed.

Jack softened. "It is difficult to know. A year or two will tell us. In over 70 percent of the cases treated, regrowth can be expected."

Fred's shoulders sank and slumped.

"Mr. Chapman, believe me when I tell you that you and your family have just been given a great gift," the doctor explained, placing his hand on Fred's chunky shoulder. "Promise me that you will live every day as if it were your last. Dance like nobody's looking. I can't promise you another day, another month, or another year. But I can promise you that in a little while she will wake up the happiest woman alive when she sees your face."

"When can we see her?"

"It will be a few hours before she is awake," Jack answered.

Over the following year, the family moved into a tiny apartment just south of the medical complex while Sonja recuperated. They wanted to stay close to Dr. Gabrielle for the Chapman family trusted no one else. After six weeks of radiation, Jack prescribed the standard PCV chemotherapy.

Jack checked the date of the operation; that was three years ago. Sonja and Fred Chapman were now waiting in an exam room.

"She's a very lucky young woman," Jack whispered to Sandy as he scanned down the test results.

"Lucky they found you," she returned.

Fred and Sonja left the office relieved. An MRI study was ordered to confirm full remission, but Jack was not worried.

Jack returned to his office, to the window. He leaned on the sill, pressing his fingers against the glass. He stood there for at least ten minutes, watching the traffic stream by below, his mind squarely on the one thing he could not cure. Complete in herself, comfortable in her skin. Thandy seemed to be conquering the world—without him.

These days, he took more weekends on call, despite having six well-trained physicians on staff and at the ready. He was resigned to this life, he thought to himself, no ready means of escape, with no clear will to simply get up and walk away, no desire to liberate Etienne from the prison she built for herself. Even so, Jack had little patience for imperfection. He'd long since tired of his wife's love affair with vodka drenched lunches. Were it not for his sons, he would be perfectly happy if she drank herself right into the grave. Divorce now felt imperfect as well. If he was guilty of depraved neglect, then so what? No one would ever charge him with abandonment. If she wanted out, he would hold the front door open and let her drag her bags to the curb.

"Ninety-nine problems but a bitch ain't one!"

Sandy brought him a no-fat vanilla latte from the café and dropped a thin stack of phone messages on his desk. He took a sip and leafed through the pink slips.

"Are you ready for the next one?"

"Let's get to it."

Working gave him less time to think about Thandy.

Chapter 3

Long after his office staff had gone for the evening, Jack finally drove out of the parking deck and into the starless night. It was well after midnight when he clicked open the wrought iron gate and pulled his 911 Turbo Porsche into the long, hedge-lined drive.

He was pleased to find Etienne sleeping, in all likelihood lulled by a mild sedative and an evening nightcap. For once she was not pacing the floors, waiting for him like a fighting cock poised for battle.

Jack left the bedroom and went down to the kitchen. He poured and drained a shot of Remy Martin Louis XIII. Better than cognac, Louie is a work of art, not unlike the priceless oils that adorned the home's foyer and living room. The idea that three generations of cellar masters had patiently and artfully created the fine liquor was nearly as intoxicating to Jack as the drink itself.

He poured another, went down to the cellar, and stripped down to his Skivvies. He sat in the damp cool basement, surrounded by old furniture and boxes, vestiges of the days when his mother welcomed the full of Atlanta society into her home.

Thoughts of Thandy crowded his mind. He didn't want to miss her, but even then, still inebriated with his own success, he could not bring himself to admit that he needed anyone. She, like the cognac, had been a perk of power. He had earned them both.

The first time he saw her ten years ago, he was fixated on the way she moved. She floated across the department store's tiled flooring as though it were a vast, marbled ballroom. She danced alone; her hips swayed beyond assorted merchandise displays until she disappeared into a fog of elegant clothing. Without thinking, he followed, trailing her by a few paces. He did not know where she had come from or where she was going.

He watched as she tended a transaction for a silver bracelet. A gift, he reasoned. He remained several yards away, just out of her line of sight and watched her. Her hands were delicate. Her buttery skin looked smooth and clear. She had wonderful, bone straight, jet-black hair that fell generously about her shoulders and flowed as if picked up by an unseen breeze. There was an inviting mystery in her full peach lips and in her pecan-shaped eyes framed by perfectly etched brows. He did not know her name, but he knew it would be divine as well. He had, in that moment, forgotten why he had come and moreover, what appointment he needed to keep. She was a worthy distraction. He didn't want to seem desperate. But desperate he was, desperate to know her, to be in her company. Shifting through a rack of shirts, he searched for an opportunity to approach.

He watched as the clerk wrapped the bracelet in sheer tissue, then boxed and handed it over. When she turned to leave, he followed.

Without thinking he said, "Go to dinner with me."

It was more of a demand than a question. He didn't even know her name.

"Well," she smiled. "I don't know . . ."

"Maybe just coffee," Jack interrupted. "I promise I won't keep you long."

"I meant to say, I do not know your name. And don't make any promises you can't keep. I'm Thandywaye Malone."

"It is good to meet you, Ms. Malone," he said, extending his hand.

"Nice to meet you."

"Jackson. And I can tell you now that I intend to break that promise. I'm going to keep you as long as you let me."

She smiled.

"My friends call me Jack. Jack Gabrielle. *Dr.* Jackson Gabrielle."

"And Mrs. Gabrielle?"

Jack was immediately confused.

"You're wearing a wedding band. I can assume that there *is* a Mrs. Gabrielle," she said, looking past his shoulder.

"There is. Well, there isn't *and* there is. We're separated," he lied. The sugar-tinged drawl deepened. "I am certain your mother will be delighted with your gift," he said, changing the subject. "She must be quite beautiful."

"It's for my daughter," she corrected in something just shy of presweetened iced tea. "Her birthday is Saturday. And yes, she is quite beautiful."

"Just like her mother."

Thandy blushed. She was quite used to strange men accosting her on the street. She'd been waved down in traffic, chased through grocery stores, and stared down to her lingerie during business meetings enough to understand that whatever she had was worth having. But Jack was different. His voice was positively melodic, yet powerfully masculine. He was the one man who looked at her as if he wanted something after tomorrow came and went.

"So you will join me for dinner, maybe Friday evening?"

She paused. "I don't know if I'm interested in a man who is, shall we say, *otherwise* encumbered."

"Don't go spending five-dollar words on me."

A grin crept up from the corner of her mouth.

"You're the doctor. You must know everything."

"In all likelihood yes," he assured. "Can you at least have dinner with a new friend?"

"How long have you been watching me?"

Ashamed, but delighted, he admitted he had indeed followed her from the moment she walked into Bloomingdale's. There was no concealing his enchantment. He was happy that she found his admission charming.

Thandy shifted feet. "There are many beautiful women in Atlanta. Do you follow all of them?"

"With my practice, I would not have the time for that," he bragged, hoping to lead her into more conversation. He felt like a schoolboy. He felt a warmth in his core he hadn't felt in years.

"Between your patients and the stalking habit you've acquired, you must keep quite busy," she joked.

"I don't have any habits. I am anything but common. And I wasn't stalking you, Miss Lady," he said plainly.

"You were so. You said it yourself. What kind of medicine?"

"I'm a surgeon and you are incredibly beautiful."

"Well, that makes you Dr. Uncommon and likely a compulsive neurotic."

"Are you always so judgmental?"

"Are you always so flirtatious?"

"Are you always so cynical?"

"Are you always so evasive?"

They laughed.

Her eyes swept past her watch, then slowly upward, moving across his face. Her skepticism had almost evaporated. Until now she had not noticed his wide, nickel-sized eyes, the heavy but pleasant bed of brows, his strong, cleft chin, the soft salt-and-pepper black curls of hair, and brilliant cocoa brown eyes. She noticed the perfectly etched lines that joined his mustache and goatee. Nervously, she pulled away. For that moment, she saw her own splendor reflected in his eyes.

He studied her again. God Himself could not have rendered a more exquisite creature. Jack couldn't help but believe that the woman standing before him, craftily evading his dinner invitation, was the sum total of all the women in the world.

"What do you do?" he asked.

She was a lawyer by training, she explained, shifting her weight, an officer with McDonough, Press, and Sweet Asset Management.

"I manage acquisitions. Sell-side."

"I am more of a buy-side kind of guy."

She grinned.

"C'mon now. That's worth a laugh," he said.

Her smile grew.

"Well, Dr. Gabrielle, I really must be going," she said, turning away. "I've got a birthday cake to bake."

"You bake, too? Do they still make women like you?"

"Baking is the least of my skills," she boasted, as he turned to follow her.

Jack knew that Etienne hadn't seen the inside of a kitchen in over a decade and didn't see the value of red velvet cake unless, of course, it was laced with vodka.

"But how will I find you again?"

"I'm listed," she threw over her shoulder.

"How will I know which . . . ?"

"Ain't but one."

"What if I can't spell it?" he laughed.

"You'll figure it out."

"Will you buy dinner if I do?"

She stopped walking. "Not a chance, Dr. Uncommon. Not a chance."

He couldn't see her face, but he knew she was still smiling. With that, he was satisfied. He would indeed seek her out, find her, and know her. If one believes his first love to be his last and his last the very first, then she had been both. He gave little thought to the *current* Mrs. Gabrielle, who was shopping with their son on the third floor. He gave little thought to the string of other beautiful women who came and went at his pleasure. Thandywaye Malone was different.

❧ ❧ ❧

His thoughts returned to the present. It would be ten years since that day in October and Thandy had made a big deal out of every anniversary of their meeting. Jack now regretted not giving her the celebration he so often told her she deserved. He hadn't been very good about birthdays, either. Never quite able to remember which day it was, Jack would invariably show up with a ten-dollar bundle of roses from the checkout line at the grocery store and a pearly smile, days late. Handling her disappointment, he'd kiss her until it was all gone. Each night as he got onto the elevator and went home to Etienne, the pangs of wanting set in.

There had been too many vacations to Sea Island, too many days when she'd come home from work after a steady eighteen hours in the office to find a sweet voice mail message, too many times when she'd called his paging system just to hear his southern lilt, too many dime-store flowers always in just the right color, too many tickle fights when both of them laughed so hard they could barely talk, too many bowls of Brunswick stew and plates of lemon pound cake ferried to the hospital when he hadn't had time for a dinner break, too many pool games when he whipped her behind because he said his foot was itching for a win only to wind up rubbing her feet as a consolation prize, too many fevered afternoons wrapped in each other's arms when neither of them wanted to be anywhere else. She rarely asked for more. They believed they had everything.

Chapter 4

Three-thirty in the morning. He couldn't pull himself to join his wife in bed. Regret raced through his mind.

Thandy had been gone several days before he noticed. He never believed she would leave him. The tear soaked voice mail messages had gone unchecked, various others left with his office ignored. He'd taken her for granted. Their last encounter replayed itself again and again in his head.

The plane from Barbados landed and he made a beeline for her condominium. The fire was already burning when he turned the key.

"Who is she?" Thandy had demanded as he stepped inside.

"Who is who?"

"Stop it, Jackson!" she shouted. "You can't just stroll in here and pretend everything is everything!" The hurt poured out of her bones like a rolling tide. "Don't you think you owe me something?"

"I don't owe anybody anything," he countered.

He believed that. Notwithstanding his trust fund, he firmly believed that he made himself through his work, his skills, his desires. He had earned everything, every single thing that the world had to offer because he had commanded it. Whatever his father had left him paled in comparison to what he'd made of it. The practice had grown exponentially under his charge. The Great Doctor Jackson Gabrielle was lord and master over the largest, most profitable surgical practice in the southeast and it was all because he had made it so.

Thandy was in his face now, shouting. "She called me!" she barked. "She called this house!"

"What?"

"She is still your wife, right? She called me last week and told me you were in Barbados! She said you were at some goddamned doctor's convention with some bitch!"

He was accustomed to coming and going as he pleased. Barbados was not the first of his indiscretions. Anguilla, St. Bart's, Nevis. There were three different medical conferences and three different women all within the span of a year. Surely, Etienne knew about them all and had never uttered a contrary word. But for Etienne to place a call to Thandy . . . she must have secretly acquired and run through his cell phone bill. He mentally counted over five hundred outbound calls in the last few months alone. But she had said nothing. In fact, these days she was playing the role of the dutiful wife. She was better than June Cleaver notwithstanding the bedtime shot of vodka. But he would deal with Etienne later. For now, he was dead set on managing the collateral damage.

"And you believe her?" he said backing up.

"Damn right I do," Thandy said, closing in on him. "Show me your fucking passport!"

"Who carries their passport around with them?"

"You do!"

His contentment with her seemed a distant memory. Her anger was unmanageable. Seeing it now, raw and unbridled, filled his chest with an unexpected pang of regret.

"Look, I haven't been to Barbados," he lied. "And there is no one else."

"Then show me the goddamned passport!" she spat.

"C'mon, Thandy. You're smarter than that," Jack said tossing his arms in the air. "She's a lunatic."

"Don't tell me she's crazy now. Just show me the damn passport," she sniffed. "We can solve this right now."

Already caught up in a space tight as a sinking coffin, he said, "You don't need to see my passport. It's me. Jack. C'mon now."

He gripped her arms and pulled her in close. Thandy snatched away. Jack grabbed her again and tugged her back to him.

"C'mon now. It's me," he said softly, edging in closer.

He kissed her tears. She buried her face in his chest as he wrapped his arms around her.

"I don't know who you are," she sobbed.

"Of course you do. We were made for this. You are the next and the *last* Mrs. Gabrielle," he crooned. "I know. I shouldn't have gone without you. But, I've missed you and only you."

He kissed her down the hall and into the master bedroom. He took off her clothes and then his own, still kissing, still caressing, still crooning as he worked his seduction. He tossed her onto the bed, worked his way through her body, lifting her firm legs around his back, grasping her meaty behind. He grasped and pushed until he could feel her anger turn to passion. He left no spot untouched, nothing undone until her wetness covered him. When it was over, he looked into her eyes expecting to see pleasure and relief. Instead, she cried like a baby as she pushed him aside.

Ah hell, he said under his breath.

Jack sniffed, threw his head back, and wished her and her tears away. He went to the bathroom and came back with a wet hand towel.

"Here, get cleaned up," he said flatly.

She didn't move. He sat on the edge of the bed and waited. Nearly an hour crept by before she muttered, "I want to know where you were. Who were you with?"

He said nothing.

"I need to hear you say it," she said.

He almost answered then caught himself. It didn't really matter; the juried conviction had long since been rendered. She'd had a full week to stew and the pot was boiling. He could say nothing.

Thandy pulled herself up in bed. He turned and looked at her.

"Go right ahead. Deny it. Deny it all, Jackie boy," she said, almost laughing, almost crying.

Not even his mother, rest her soul, had called him Jackie.

"Misery loves company," he sighed under his breath.

"Misery? Yes Jackson. I am miserable," she said kicking him through the blankets. "God damn it! I am fucking mis-er-able! Miserable! I gave you my life! And what is it that you give me in return? A bunch of empty promises?" she shrieked. "C'mon Jack! If I'm just a piece of ass, shouldn't you write a check before you leave?"

"I did that already," he said with controlled anger. "Look around you, sweetness."

"Fuck this damn house! Maybe I should march along Peachtree Street, wearing a sandwich board that says 'Cat for Sale'!"

"Do what you have to do. I didn't force you to pull hundred-hour weeks or volunteer like a storm trooper for Sloane's campaign."

"Oh, now I'm to blame?" she sneered.

On the rare occasion when Mr. Elijah, his favorite bartender, said a narrow word edgewise, he once told Jack the story of two farmers, one coming to visit the other on an especially hot summer day. A hound dog lay on the plank wood decking howling as if being tortured with a hot poker.

"What's wrong with your hound?" the visitor asked.

The dog's owner kept sipping a tall, cold glass of iced tea, seemingly unbothered by his dog's constant wails and moans.

"Her belly is perched on a bent rusty nail," the farmer replied finally. "That dern nail is digging her in her side."

Still the dog wailed as if Jesus himself had forsaken her.

A short time later, the first farmer's family returned from church. The visitor thought for certain the wife or one of the towheaded children would stop and take at least a bit of pity on the aging mutt. All entered the house without so much as taking a second look at the crying hound. The visitor was perplexed, but he'd seen enough.

"Well, why don't she just get up? She can walk, can't she?" he pressed.

The farmer sighed deeply, but said nothing until the visitor begged for an answer. The farmer looked at his neighbor curiously and said, "Yeah, she can walk sure enough. She's got four able legs. And I imagine she could get on along if she wanted to. But, I guess it don't bother her enough."

Thandy was on her feet now. With her fists thrust down to her sides, she continued to demand the truth. Jack was thinking about the wailing dog and Thandy's pouting was starting to feel like a bent, rusty nail. He wanted a shower and a fresh pair of trousers. She was still screaming an unintelligible list of demands when he got up from the bed. He had gotten no further than the Italian-stone tiled bathroom floor—the very floor he had demanded ripped up and replaced when the cheap linoleum that once covered it didn't meet his standards—when her fists came crashing down on his back like a roll of thunder before a hard rain.

"You bastard!" she screamed, beating her clinched hands against his back. "You don't even think me worthy of a good lie! Get out! You bastard! You fucking bastard! You thieving fucking bastard! Get out!"

He turned, pushed through the wave of falling fists, and grabbed her shoulders tight. She shook violently. He embraced her whole body. They fell to the floor before she stilled. Pinning her to the stonework, he stared into her face.

"Look what you've done," she sobbed. "Look what you've done to me," she cried.

"We cannot live this way. I won't live this way," he said softly.

"But, there is no one else, Thandy. This isn't about you. It isn't about me. It's about us," he consoled. He half hoped she wouldn't show up in divorce court as a plaintiff's witness. She held his life in her hands. The others could be explained away, but ten years with a woman like Thandy and any judge worth his salt would strip him of everything he owned.

"Etienne would just love it if you walked away. That's why she called, baby. She wanted this to happen. She'll do anything to tear us apart."

"What do you want from me?" she cried.

"You didn't tell her anything, did you?"

"Nothing she didn't already know."

"I just want us," he lied. "You have to know that," he said as he stroked her hair.

"But there is no us," she whimpered. "It's just you and everything else. When will I be enough? When will I get to be first?"

"You're first every day," he smiled.

"I'm not enough for you," she whispered.

"You don't believe that," he said. "You are my first and my last," he said kissing her face.

He lifted her and the unfortunate pack of lies up and into the cradle of his arms, then carried them back to the bed. Jack adjusted a pillow beneath her head and covered her with a knitted afghan. She wanted something he couldn't give her.

"If you must know, I did go to the conference," he said. "But there was no one with me. I went alone," he lied. "I needed some space."

"I thought you wanted me in your space," she said softly. "When did you stop needing me?"

He sat at her side with his head in his hands. What exactly did she expect from him? She had a million-dollar condo and a brand new SLK 350 was parked in the deck. Whatever she was, he had paid for it in full.

అ అ అ

Two weeks later, after at first believing she had simmered down and come to her senses and then later in desperation ringing her phone off the hook, their mutual best friend and gubernatorial candidate Sloane Faulkner delivered the news.

"Bruh, didn't you get her messages?" Sloane asked. "Get me off this speaker phone."

"What messages?" he asked, picking up the line, distracted by his charts.

"Thandy said she left several, but you didn't return them."

Sloane had been their only friend, the only one who knew the full of their relationship and understood.

"Man, I've been running back and forth to the hospital. I've had three surgeries today. Besides, after that trip to Barbados, 'Etty the Terrible' has me on lockdown. Thandy was pissed off, but she'll cool down. That's just the way of it."

"You told them you went down there with Angel?"

"Are you kidding? The first rule is to deny. The second rule is to deny. And the third one is . . ."

"I know. Deny," Sloane said with disapproval lacing his words.

"I don't know how Etienne found out. Hell, she never said shit to me about it. But Thandy said Etienne called her."

"You're shitting me?"

Jack swiveled his chair to look out the window.

"No, by the time I got over to the condo she was ready to kick my ass."

"Lord, Lord, Lord. Doc, when are you going to figure out what you've got? Thandy is some kind of special. You're a fool to let her go."

"Special? That girl nearly tore my eyes out. Look, I've got one more in surgery before I can close out the day," he said, turning to a thick stack of medical charts. "Then I gotta get home. Etienne's got quite a show going on right now. The next thing you know she'll be making me blueberry pancakes dressed in a red corset, fish nets, and stilettos."

He looked to his watch. He had less than ten minutes to scrub for the next procedure. The charge nurse threw him silent signals that it was time. Jack ignored her. His shifted his weight to his left foot and blew out a gust.

"Jack, this is me you're talking to. You aren't going to let her walk out like that, are you? Remember, this ain't no casual honey dip we're talking about."

"Who says it's not?" he sighed. "If she wants to act like the rest of them, then let's see if she can live with the consequences. I can't afford to waste my time thinking about it."

"Are you trying to convince me or you? I don't know a man on this planet who'd let her walk out. I certainly wouldn't."

The nurse shoved another chart under his nose. Jack twirled his eyes around the iridescent lights in the ceiling and said, "Then you go get her. I don't have time for all that drama."

"Angel is that good, huh?"

"I'm not saying that, but I'm not signing up for another war. As for Angel, she's the honey dip, something to break up the monotony. Nothing complicated. She just screws my brains out and I go home."

Sloane took a deep breath and said, "Listen, doc. I didn't want to be the one to tell you but Thandy is going to Chicago."

"So?"

Ninety-nine problems but a bitch ain't one!

"So, she's moving," Sloane continued. "It's for good. She got some big job with Campbell-Perkins, I think. She said she isn't coming back."

Jack was silent at first. He stopped fumbling through the charts and tossed up a single finger to the nurse who was pacing the station. *One minute.*

"I don't know what she told you, but Thandywaye Malone isn't leaving me, man. She can't. I know that girl better than she knows herself. She could stand to grow up. She can't go running off every time the breeze doesn't blow her way. She knows what she signed up for. I was married the day she met me."

"Ten years is a long time."

"Now you're on her side? What did she expect? I can't just walk away from my house."

"People do it every day of the week."

"I'm trying to do right by my family."

"And you think that means letting your wife drink herself to death."

"When'd you start giving a shit about Etienne?" Jack said, feeling himself get heated. "I'm going to ask you one more time. Whose side are you on?"

"You didn't know she was gone, did you?"

Jack was silent.

"How long has it been?" Sloane pressed.

"Two weeks."

"Don't be a fool, Jack. Go get yourself a copy of *The New York Times*."

"For what?"

"Just take a look at the business section."

"Is there a new voter poll out? What do the numbers look like today?" he said referring to the upcoming race.

"You know I never listen to the numbers. I run every day like I'm coming from behind. I'm giving it all I've got."

"You're going to be Georgia's first black governor."

"From your lips to God's ears. But you get yourself a copy of the paper."

Jack spent the next three hours resecting a dime-sized growth from Mr. Kilpatrick's neck. The surgery would not likely spare his patient's life and this troubled Jack more than Thandy's departure. The squamous cell carcinoma had metastasized into the lining of his mouth, nose, and throat. Kilpatrick had two or three months if he was lucky. Removing the growth would at least make it easier for him to breathe.

Jack almost forgot about buying the newspaper. He went down to the gift shop and bought a copy just before closing time. There on the front page of the business section was a color photo of

Thandy dressed in an ivory suit with her arms folded across her chest like she was Queen of the Known Universe. Jack read the entire story twice before he got to the elevator. When the door opened onto the parking deck, Jack broke out running. Out of breath, he hopped into his car, gunned the engine, and sped out of the lot.

She was gone.

Chapter 5

They left day before yesterday, doc," the doorman said. "The moving van pulled out of here this morning."

The doorman discreetly folded the hundred dollar bill and slipped it in the breast coat pocket of his suit jacket. He reached into the bell stand, handed Jack the sealed envelope and a set of car keys Thandy left for him.

"She left this for you."

She knew he would come. Jack thanked the doorman and left. He got in his car and opened it. Inside were the deed to the condominium and a notarized quit claim deed, transferring her share of the ownership back to him, and a certified check for the estimated rent she would have paid had it not been a gift. Thandy was giving back the house free and clear. On a Post-it note she scribbled the words "Thank you." The condo and the car had been gifts—gifts she no longer wanted.

Now alone in the quiet of the cellar, Jack sat in a Victorian walnut nursing chair. He reared back on the cabriole legs weighing what was left of his life. His mind welled with a deep fog of regret and longing for something he could not name. He settled further into the chair, stretching his lengthy legs out before him. The full of his life cascaded down like a rushing waterfall. The century-old chair that once graced the upper parlor was still sturdy, if not a bit dusty from its decades'-long abandonment in the cellar.

He scanned the dim room, lit only by a trail of light from the top of the staircase. The Crosley entertainer he loved as a boy collected dust atop a satinwood demilune table. He wondered if the record player still worked and set about looking for the stack of 78 rpm albums he knew for certain his father had saved. He found the cache of records, in their original sleeves, neatly stacked in a box beneath a lowboy. He selected one of the LPs, blew away the dust, wiped what remained with his handkerchief, and placed it on the turntable. He dug into his pockets for change. He plucked out three nickels and stacked them carefully on the arm to hold it steady, lest the recording skip. His father taught him the trick when he was a boy.

Billy Eckstine's rich warm baritone voice floated from the speaker.

"I wanna be loved with inspiration . . ."

It was better that Thandy had gone, he thought. Better for her. Better for him, he tried to convince himself. Jack explored the room for still more forgotten treasures, kicking back cobwebs and tossing back white sheets that covered antique furniture. He found a silver three-armed candelabrum and lit the wicks to aid his sight. His favorite baseball bat leaned against the wall. Running his fingers along the wood, he remembered every nick and scratch. It was the very bat he used to belt a three-run homer over the wall at Piedmont Park in the summer of 1973. As the ball sailed beyond the east field, the little brown boys rounded the bases. His parents cheered from the wooden bleachers as Jack stomped his feet on home plate. The baseball diamond was now gone, returned to the field of green it had once been. But his memories survived. He grabbed the choke with both hands and took a swing just to see if he still had it. The bat cut through the air like a sword. He felt his power trail from his limbs into the tip of the wood. The sweet spot. Right then, he wanted to be ten years old again.

Searching still, he discovered a locked Louis Vuitton trunk wrapped in hand-sewn quilts. The suffocating, musty smell of mildewed fabric swirled around his nose. The trunk was covered in leather with the signature monogram logo of its maker and trimmed in wood and metal. He tinkered with the lock, his mind set on discovering what was inside. After a few moments, he gave up and returned to the nursing chair. Every soul has a match, every heart specifically deep with wanting. Every lock has a key, he thought. The Fabulous Mr. B's sweet melancholy voice crackled from the Crosley.

"*. . . and I insist the world owes me a loving.*"

He could fathom no good reason for staying, but he could not find peace with a woman at war with herself, he measured. He had no remedy for her maladies, most of which could be found in the bottom of a dirty Belvedere martini or a cup of bourbon-laced coffee.

Etienne's one cardinal sin had been to love Jack's money, to adore his position in society more than she did him. Being Mrs. Gabrielle came with privileges. A cattle call would yield dozens willing to stand in line for the chance to take her place. If need be, Jack knew, they'd stand naked in a snowstorm.

Chapter 6

Yvetta Malone still lives in the modest white brick house where she raised her family, on Delmar Street in Winston-Salem, North Carolina. The long narrow gravel road is now paved and the driveway has a new coat of black asphalt. Traffic is frequent, but tolerable. Children still play out in the middle of the avenue. Peering over her morning paper, she often amuses herself in their merriment from her painted concrete stoop. Mrs. Malone knows their mothers and their mothers' mothers since she is a retired substitute schoolteacher. Most were her students at one time or another and every little brown face is familiar. She knows where they go to school and what kind of grades they get. She knows when some get into trouble and when the girls are keeping company too long with a certain boy or another. The children always turn their kickball game away from her yard so a stray ball won't wander over her chain-link fence. They don't want any trouble getting it back. They call her Mrs. Malone, as she prefers. Generally speaking, the children behave themselves whenever Mrs. Malone is out on the porch. If something goes amiss, they know she'll come out to the street, swat the aggressors on the behind, and then promptly call their mothers.

Yvetta mostly kept herself in the house these days. But at

least one morning a week, she'd get outside in short britches, work gloves, and a polka-dot head scarf to tend to the spray rose-bushes. She had a mental list of things that needed to be done. The house and the black shutters could use a fresh coat of paint. She figured she would get around to it next spring when money might be better. There is the matter of a dead hardwood leaning too close to the back of the house and the gas stove needs replacing. The paint job would have to wait. The tree needed to be cut down, chopped up, and hauled off before the next storm.

Jesse Fields from around the way had offered his hand with the lawn and maybe even would see after that tree. But Yvetta was dead set on mowing the lawn herself and told him the tree was her problem to see after. Everybody in the neighborhood knew she didn't care for menfolk in her yard. She told him more than once that she didn't need any looking after. Still Fields came by every Saturday and leaned on the gatepost for small talk.

"How are you getting along there, Miss Malone?" Mr. Fields would call from the sidewalk.

"Mrs. Malone," she always corrected. "And I'm doing just dandy, thank you," she'd say and look away.

It always started that way. He kept talking until she either came down from the porch and joined him at the fence or went inside and forgot he was there. When she did come out to the gate, they talked about the various comings and goings in town, including Maya Angelou's arrival at Wake Forest University. When she'd had enough, Yvetta politely excused herself and went back to doing nothing. He'd turn on his heels and head back home. It went on that way for two years or better. Nothing ever changed.

Mrs. Grace Goins still lived across the street, though she wasn't home much these days. She explained one Saturday morning over coffee and sweet biscuits that she needed to be over in Wilmington more often to see after her baby sister, who was recovering from diabetes surgery. She'd lost her foot to sugar and needed more than a little help getting around. Yvetta promised to look after the house when Grace was away. Other than that or a quick hand of cards with Eunice Rivers, who lived just a few houses up, Yvetta was happy enough. Every Sunday after church, Yvetta would make her way out to the senior home to see after her father.

At ninety-seven, Henry Tecumseh "Cump" Cole was a wily old cooter who had a touch of high blood pressure and a little sugar himself, but other than that he was in good health. Progressive senility was the worst of it, though everybody thought he could remember everything he wanted to. On most days, Cump could tell you he had eight children, four of them still living, and had been married just once to undoubtedly the most beautiful woman in all of North Carolina. He would jet out of the house on a moment's notice to go for a walk. Invariably, he'd get lost and one of the neighbor kids would fetch and bring him back. For a while, Yvetta and her young anointed deputies were able to keep up with him.

The last time he got out, Yvetta got a call from the Greyhound bus terminal in Rock Hill, South Carolina. It seemed he'd convinced the driver that he lived there and needed to get home. When nobody showed up for him, the ticket agent searched his pockets for identification. Directory assistance gave the attendant a phone number on Delmar Street. On Yvetta's instruction, the ticket agent put Cump on a bus headed back to Winston-Salem and told the driver not to let him off until they got there. He got off the bus mumbling something about going to Atlanta to see his grandbaby. Although she was relieved to have him back, that was the end of it. Yvetta reluctantly signed him into the senior home for safekeeping.

Most Sundays she would sit with him and watch television in the recreation room. Glad to see her, but not quite remembering who she was, Cump talked in buckshots like he would to any other perfect stranger. In all of his living days, he'd never met a stranger. He'd ramble on about Dan Rather, who he referred to only as the new fair-haired boy on the nightly news, and how he couldn't hold a candle to Walter Cronkite. *And that's the way it is.* Cump was always dissatisfied with the food and thought his room was too cold.

"Can you get them to give me some real food? I'm sick and tired of dern Jell-O. It ain't natural to feed anybody anything green that don't grow out the ground. And I need a lock for my closet. Somebody's been snooping around in there. I know they done stole some of my clothes. You see that, Myrtle, you tell her to get on up here and see about her husband. Somebody done run off with his clothes!"

Her mother, Myrtle Cole, passed away ten years ago. Yvetta found no benefit to reminding her father about that. She'd already checked his inventory of slacks and button-down shirts a dozen times or more, but never found anything amiss. Sometimes she borrowed a steam iron from the orderly and pressed out some of his slacks. He liked them crisp and tidy even if sometimes he couldn't remember his own name. Yvetta bought him a new pair of shoes and promised to get him a lock, if only to give him peace of mind. Like her own husband, Simon, Cump had been a postal worker after a long stint as a porter on the railroad. He amused Yvetta with stories of segregated sleeping and dining cabins, even though he sometimes couldn't remember what he had for breakfast that morning.

"I was a good rail man," he told her. "When they wanted to form a union, I said 'no, sir.' I knew the company would just as soon cut us loose and find somebody else to do the job. Thirty years, I rode the line. I done seen every part of the country from top to bottom. I met my Myrtle out there. Sweet, baby sweet she was, sweet as Vidalia onions."

Yvetta beamed. She enjoyed her father's stories.

"They didn't come no prettier than your mama. I tell you the truth. We got married right out there at Mt. Sinai. That was a day. Your uncle Harold was my best man. Crazy Harry. That's what they called him, you know? Only time he ever wore a suit was to my wedding and to his own funeral. They buried him in that suit.

You know that tan seersucker I got? Well, that's what I want you to bury me in. Tell that preacher man over at Mt. Sinai to lay me out good. But tell him not to preach too long. You know he sure can talk the angels out of heaven, but you tell him not to preach on me too long."

"Yes sir," Yvetta answered.

"You find that seersucker and press it out good."

"Yes sir."

"Go easy on the starch."

Yvetta knew the suit, if she could find it, would be too large. Cump was down to a rail thin 120 pounds, soaking wet with bricks in his pockets. He went on talking. He didn't take two breaths at a time.

"Gal, it smells like piss in here. They oughta clean this place up. What they need is a bucket of pine cleaner for them toilets and some ammonia for this here floor. I told that gal out there to give me the mop," he said pointing down the hallway. "I'll get this place smelling like daisies."

Clearly satisfied with himself, he asked Yvetta about her husband, Simon.

"When's he gone make it by here?"

"He's gone now."

"Gone where?"

"Daddy, Simon passed on five years ago."

"That so? Well, I'm sorry to know that," he said as if he'd heard for the first time right then. "He sure was a good man." He welled up and blew out a gust from his nose.

The news that his Myrtle had gone on too would certainly bring tears. "Yes sir, he was," Yvetta said instead.

"I remember the day you brought him home. He was standing out there in the yard sweating like a prostitute in the church house. I told him it was all right to come on in the house. Your mama had to go out there and get him. We lived out on Euclid Avenue back then. He took off his hat and sat down on the couch. Didn't move two inches the whole time he was there.

Wasn't no need in him being afraid of me. He was from good people. I got him on at the post office."

"And we're glad for it, Daddy."

Yvetta was both amazed and tickled with his selective memory. Cump could not often remember where he was going, but he certainly knew where he had been.

"Them girls of yours look just like him. But they've got my eyes," he beamed.

"Yvonne is a school teacher," Yvetta reminded him.

"Is that right? What's the other one's name?"

"That's your grandbaby, Thandy, Daddy."

"Oh, I knew that. I just wanted to see if you remembered. Than-DE-way!" he said almost singing his granddaughter's name. "Oh, I just like to call her name and watch her come running. She still likes butterscotch candy, don't she? I used to keep a pocket full of butterscotch just for her. Wintertime will be along soon. You know how she loves snow, my January girl. Maybe she'll come to see me."

Yvetta lost her smile.

"I'm sure she will, Daddy."

Yvetta was proud of Yvonne. She was married now with children of her own. She took a teaching job and followed her husband, Rich Colbert, over to Charlotte where he was doing real nice for himself, selling advertising at a local television station. The couple saved enough for a decent down payment on a lovely ranch on a quiet street. They had two children, six-year-old Jada and baby Amber. The Colberts led busy, orderly lives and Simon would have approved. Rich coached Little League baseball and Yvonne was a volunteer with an adult literacy program. They churched every Sunday at Friendship Baptist. Yvetta hadn't been over to see them since early spring, she lamented. *They must be getting big now,* she thought. Little Jada seemed to pick up two inches every time Yvetta visited. But, she didn't like driving alone without Simon.

After five years of mourning her precious Simon, time seemed to move along a little bit slower, creeping by quiet and slow like a ladybug. The house was long since paid for and the postal service kindly sent the widow pension benefits every third of the month. Other than visits from her best friend Grace, there was little other excitement. Coming to see her father made Sundays go by better.

An attendant announced dinner: pot roast, steamed butter corn, and iced tea.

"What's for dessert? We ain't having no more dern Jell-O, are we?"

"Not tonight, Mr. Cole," the nurse assured. "We got lemon pound cake."

"Hot damn!" he exclaimed, scooting his wheelchair toward the dining room.

Yvetta followed him to his table, kissed his forehead, and left him eating.

She thought about Thandy the whole way home. She'd just gotten in the door when she heard the phone on the kitchen wall ringing.

"Mrs. Malone? I'm sorry to disturb you. This is Dr. Gabrielle."

"What is it, Jackson?" Her voice was curt. She leaned against the arched door frame and asked, "What are you calling me for?"

"I've been trying to reach Thandywaye," he tried to explain. "I wondered if you could give me a home phone number for her. I seem to have misplaced it."

"I see." She didn't believe a word. "You're asking me?"

"Again, ma'am. I'm sorry to disturb you. But it's important."

"Life or death, huh?" Her sarcasm was palpable.

"You could say that."

"I ain't nobody's fool, Dr. Gabrielle," Yvetta said, raising her voice. "If my daughter wanted you to know where she was at, she would've told you as much. To tell you the truth, I'm glad you can't find her. The Good Lord ain't never gone bless what you were doing."

"Again, I'm sorry . . ."

"You most certainly are," she said cutting him off. "If you call my house again, I'll call the police on you. You hear me?"

Before he could answer, she laid the phone down on the receiver and went back to the porch. Thandy hadn't told her mother about Chicago either. Yvetta read about it in the paper like everybody else.

She'll get tired of running and come on home, Yvetta wished as she looked out onto the street filled with neighborhood children playing kickball.

Chapter 7

The next night, as the August sun was going down and the moon crept up over the horizon, the neighborhood kids were still playing outside on the asphalt. They jumped double Dutch and roller-skated down the middle of the street. Yvetta slipped off her lace-up walking shoes and sat on steps leaning against the metal railings. She remembered the gone days when her own girls played under the same streetlights.

She thought about driving up to Chicago, but quickly put away the notion. She didn't even know where her daughter lived, let alone how to get to Illinois. She could take a plane, but she hadn't been on one in years. Not since that crash in Florida when the shattered plane spilled across the Everglades like somebody tipped over a can of garbage. One hundred and ten people died in the dark swamp water. That was 1996, but it might as well have been that afternoon. The Buick in the driveway was ten years old, but didn't have more than six thousand miles on it. She'd never driven any further than Charlotte without Simon. She'd get lost once she crossed the Carolina border, she told herself. *What if she turns me away?*

Fresh back from Wilmington, Grace stopped by to see about her friend.

"How's your daddy doing?" she asked, padding up the stoop.

"He's keeping," Yvetta said through the screen door. "Still crazy as a jaybird, but he's keeping. Nutty as a dern fruitcake."

Yvetta stood up and swung open the screen door and waved her in. They shuffled inside the small living room and sat on the paisley print sofa. Grace had her own list of troubles on her mind. Her son, Jeremiah, was in the state penitentiary doing time for armed robbery. The sheriff had come looking for her daughter, Hope, for a string of bad checks. Grace pointed them straight out to the lean-to flophouse where she was holed up with friends. Grace hoped maybe they'd lock her up and she would get clean.

"Daddy was asking after Thandy yesterday evening," Yvetta said casually. "I pray every night that she has finally come to her senses."

"I know what you're saying, Vetta. These children these days ain't like we was. It's a different day, don't you know. My Wendell is turning over in his grave, I know that. We try to teach them right from wrong, but that don't mean they listening."

"I ain't nothing about no dern infidelity, Grace," she said. "She chose that life when she could've had better. That Thandy could have her pick of good decent men. What does she want with an alley cat like Jack Gabrielle anyhow? You remember when she brought him up here, parading him around like a show horse? That took some kind of nerve bringing that man into her daddy's house. My husband wasn't even in the ground good. She didn't need to tell me he was married. I could smell it on him. Simon wouldn't have stood for that and she knows it."

She turned her head to the wall above the sofa. It was lined with family photos in frames she bought from JCPenney. There was one of Thandy when she was twelve years old, had a wide toothy smile, and still thought the sun didn't come up until her daddy got out of bed in the morning.

"Vetta, we all want better for our children. At least she ain't on drugs. My Wendell left here never knowing what Hope was up to. I guess I'm glad for that. Thankful for the small things."

"Wendell sure was a good man," Yvetta said.

She went for coffee, poured two cups, and set out some cream and sugar. The women traded more stories about their children's misdeeds. Grace remembered when the trouble started with Thandy when she was fourteen. The whole neighborhood heard her screaming for mercy. *No need in beating no child like that*, she thought to herself at the time. *Ain't no good gone come of that.* Silently, she was glad Thandy found a way out and wondered if Yvetta had any hard feelings about it. Nobody, herself included, would even think to intervene. She wondered now if that cut on Thandy's face ever healed good.

As she sipped her coffee, which she took drowned in sugar and heavy cream, she remembered the night she heard Yvetta yelling from clear across the street.

"God don't like ugly!" Yvetta shrieked. "You bring evil into your house then you deserve every piece of sorrow you get. You got to go to the Lord first, ask His forgiveness, and then you can come to me."

Grace had sat tight-lipped out on her stoop across the street and watched Yvetta throw clothes onto the front lawn. Thandy had taken up with a man she hardly knew, a man ten years her senior who had a pocket full of money and promised her the world. Anything was better than a sleepy life in Winston-Salem, she thought at the time.

"You are dead to me! You hear that, girl?" her mother shouted down the driveway. "You are dead to me!"

In the early years, Grace knew life for the Malone family was mostly unremarkable. Simon came home every day at six, just in time for dinner. After an invariably hearty and rib-sticking meal, he always took to his easy chair for the evening news. They went to dinner at the Ponderosa Steak House every Wednesday night after church services. The girls were expected to have the chores done and their homework ready for inspection each evening. The rules were clear: be selective about your friends, focus on your studies, keep your legs closed, and clean your room like an army barracks. The house smelled like lemon furniture polish and pine cleaner. The weekends were saved for more chores and more churching. Thandy's grandparents, Cump and Myrtle, always made it by for Sunday supper.

"A good education will take you anywhere you want to go," Cump often told Thandy. "An idle mind is the devil's playground. Don't you get on his swing set."

Always prone to please, Thandy's sister, Yvonne, who was two years older and the most average-looking girl on the planet, took heed and later won a full scholarship to Duke University. Living in her sister's perfect shadow, Thandy had been rebellious from the start. She craved her parents' attention, which seemed reserved for Yvonne. By the time she was a freshman she was bored to tears with her class work and defied her father's nightly curfew. On Friday nights, she frequented the parking lot of a local fast-food restaurant and smoked marijuana with less than desirable friends. At fourteen, she was arrested on assorted charges including violating the city mandated curfew for minors and drug possession. The family posted bond and awaited a court date. Embarrassed and angry, that night at home Simon beat Thandy with a leather strap until he was dog tired. Beads of sweat rained down like black pearls, but he kept swinging until the metal belt buckle caught her in the temple. Blood gushed and ran down the side of her face.

"Mama make him stop! Please make him stop," she pleaded.

Her mother looked on in silence.

"You earned every lick," she told her daughter that night. "We ain't raised you to get out there like that. You got to get your mind right, child. Your daddy works too hard for you to throw it away like this. I'll eat dirt before I let a child of mine disrespect this house. Get some peroxide on that cut and wrap it up. It'll heal."

Thandy went to her room and started packing her clothes, first folding then throwing in anything that would fit. She bounced up and down on the plastic red Samsonite cases until she could latch the locks.

"Those are *my* suitcases," Yvetta protested. "If you leave here tonight, you ain't leaving with nothing that's mine. You better get yourself some paper bags."

Yvetta dumped out the suitcases and started hauling her daughter's clothes out the front door.

Thandy went to school the day after the beating wearing long sleeves and pants to hide the whelps and bruises. Nothing could cover the open wound on her face.

"I gotta get out of here," she told her sister as they walked to the school yard. "I can't go back, but I ain't got no where to go."

"It's your fault," Yvonne dismissed. "You keep cutting up like that and he'll keep giving it to you."

Thandy was too scared to go home and too scared not to. So she returned. She lay awake at night, too terrified to close her eyes, trying to hold on to better days when her daddy would take her to the park and push her in the swings. She remembered how he used to wait at the bottom of the metal slide when she came barreling down. She wanted to make homemade chocolate ice cream with her mother and stay up watching black and white John Wayne movies while her mother braided her hair. She didn't know the people who slept in the bedroom down the hall. Thandy couldn't stand to look up at the framed picture of Jesus that hung in the living room over the floor model Zenith television set.

The following week, Thandy was back in the same parking lot with the same load of friends. They laughed about the court dates. The group grew quiet when Thandy pulled back her hair and showed them the gash. She pulled up her shirt, revealing the whelps left by her father's thrashing. Molly Fiveashe, a pot-smoking whore that only showed up to school once or twice a week and who everybody knew had been in and out of foster care three times already, advised Thandy to call the welfare office. "They'll lock him up," Molly said as she rolled another one between her bony fingers. Monty Boykins shoved his hands in the front pockets of his washed-out Levi's, leaned against the hood of his car, and said, "You can come and stay with me."

Thandy left home for good that night. She was fifteen. She

liked his small apartment. She felt free with him and told him so. Monty was tall, with generous looks, and twenty-five. He worked double shifts at his father's Quik Wash, a job that paid well, and took classes three nights a week at Wake Forest.

Thandy was jailbait and Monty knew the crazy African would waste no time pressing charges. So, for weeks he never touched her. Not for the lack of wanting, but out of fear. Rather, he watched the beautiful young girl with long raven hair sleep peacefully. She seemed to need every moment of solace he could give her. Each morning, he would change the bandage on her face and sooth peroxide and cocoa butter on her back and arms, and tell her everything would be okay. He was gentle, and his hands loving.

"Don't you want me?" she asked one morning.

"I do, but . . ."

"But what?"

"You're on the pill, right?"

"Yeah," she lied.

He pulled her in close, taking her face into his hands. She'd never been kissed like that before. She felt his excitement rubbing against her belly. Monty abruptly pulled away.

"What's wrong?"

"Nothing," he said. "Nothing. As long as you're sure you want to do it."

Their relationship was the worst kept secret in Winston-Salem. Yvetta was furious. Her daughter's storied sex life of shacking up with a grown man was being casually tossed around the teachers' lounge. She stormed out and went straight down to the Quik Wash. She threatened to send Monty to jail for contributing to the delinquency of a minor, kidnapping, and anything else she could think of. She looked the young man square in the eye and promised to bring him up on rape charges. Simon Malone went to the high school and dragged his daughter out of a classroom. He beat her with his fists all the way to the car.

"You're a drug addict! You won't go whoring around here and soil my family name like that!"

Thandy fell to the pavement. Her father picked her up by the hair and threw her into the passenger seat of his Buick. The gash tore open. Blood spilled onto the floorboard.

"I'm going to send that bastard to jail," Simon told his daughter.

The juvenile court judge ordered counseling and probation for running away and truancy. She was four months pregnant and desperately trying to hide it. Rather than face her parents with the news, Monty and Thandy decided to run away to Atlanta, where he had family. Monty emptied his savings account, put a down payment on a new Chevrolet Cavalier and headed off south with his new family. He would do anything for Thandy. Everything they owned was in the U-Haul hitched to the bumper. It was dark when they arrived in the city of hills. The Atlanta skyline was more beautiful than any she'd ever seen. Black people drove fancy cars and lived in fine houses. Even the mayor was black.

"That's how we are going to live," Monty promised, pointing to a passing young black couple driving a new Mercedes. "I don't want my wife to worry about anything."

He hadn't proposed marriage before, but Thandy immediately thought it was a good idea. She wanted her baby to have her father's name. They married two weeks later partly because they were in love, but mostly because Monty didn't want to face charges in North Carolina. Her parents learned of the union when Simon Malone tried to swear out a warrant. The sheriff told them that he couldn't list Thandy as a runaway because according to Georgia law once married she was no longer a minor. Simon Malone pressed the issue. He went down to the sheriff's office every day for three days straight. But the sheriff refused to file for a warrant. He and everybody else had heard the stories about Simon Malone's public floggings of his daughter and were silently glad the little girl had run away.

Montana was born five months later.

෴ ෴ ෴

It wasn't long before Grace and Yvetta were belly laughing again. This time it was about Eunice Rivers's new boyfriend.

"He's just after her insurance check," Yvetta commented like she knew firsthand.

"He'll be long gone when it dries up," Grace chortled.

Seems Eunice was too busy now to play cards. The young buck couldn't be more than thirty, they decided with a giggle.

"They say he's working hard for that money. You don't ever see a frown on Eunice's face."

"I guess she deserves a little something in return," Grace sniffed. "I see Fields is making his way around here."

"He don't want nothing," Yvetta dismissed. "Ain't nothing to it. Just talking mess, that's all."

"Fields is good looking for a man his age."

"He ain't good looking enough to get in *your* fence."

Grace pulled herself out of the crack in the sofa, straightened her floral print skirt, and said, "He can come in my fence any-time."

She was well into her sixties, but Grace still had a set of firm breasts and a big smile, both of which she left wide open so any available man might see the welcome mat.

"Shoot, you can have him. I ain't nothing about no seventy-two-year-old."

"Seventy-one," Grace corrected.

"Don't make no difference. He's got a hump in his back! Dirty old men will give you worms!" Yvetta teased.

"Ain't nothing dirty about Jesse Fields. He sure does have eyes for you, and you ain't no spring chicken yourself."

Yvetta sighed. Sixty-five was right around the corner. She'd make her way down to the Social Security office to fill out the pa-perwork.

"Every woman has her needs," Grace said. "Including you."

"My Simon saw after every need, want, and desire I might ever have."

"Don't take offense, Vetta, but Simon is gone now. Wendell,

too. They'd want us to have a little piece of sunshine in our lives."

"Ain't no sun shining out of Jesse Fields."

"You just let him in that there fence first. *Then* you tell me how much sun he's got left in him," Grace said. She rose up from the chair a bit, straightened her dress beneath her generous behind, and sat back down.

"I will do no such thing," Yvetta said. "This is still Simon Malone's house."

"This here is your house, Vetta. I'm just saying Simon would want you to have something for yourself." Grace paused for a moment, then said, "You ought to go on up to Chicago and see after Thandy. I bet she needs her mama right now."

Yvetta let her words fall on the floor. She hadn't told her friend about the call from Jack. She wouldn't admit that Thandy hadn't called or been home since her father's funeral five years ago. She didn't have to tell Grace anything she didn't already know.

"Did you see that story in the paper about the colored boy running for governor down in Georgia?"

"I did," Yvetta said. "He can't win."

"Too close to call."

"They call up white folks and ask 'um how they'll vote. They ain't got to tell the truth. Ain't no white man gonna let a colored boy be his governor."

"That Osaka boy won that race up in Illinois. That's saying something ain't it?"

"Obama," Yvetta corrected. "He ain't no China-man."

"Sounds too much like bin Laden for me, but you go on and say what you want. This is still the south. It wasn't that long ago that my daddy and his daddy couldn't get a glass of Coca-Cola at Gresham's soda fountain. But, they say it is close."

"They always say that. It ain't nothing but a setup. Ain't no way they gonna let a black man run all of Georgia. Times ain't changed that much," Grace huffed definitively.

"He's fool enough to run. They might be fool enough to elect him."

Grace eyed her friend with concern. "Vetta," she said, "you know it's been a whole lot of years now. You can't tell me you don't want to see your grandbaby. I bet Montana is a beautiful young woman now."

"She's seventeen and probably just like her mama," Yvetta dismissed. "A hard head makes for a soft behind. I see all the grandbabies I need to see right over there in Charlotte. Yvonne is teaching now, you know."

"I know."

"Of course, you do. Don't nothing happen around here that you don't know about."

"You've only told me eighty dozen times. And I ain't no gossip."

"I ain't saying you are. I'm just saying you're better than the Sunday paper they throw in the yard."

"That's some big job Thandy's got herself. You should be real proud."

"I hope she don't go back to Atlanta. That man had a way with my child. I hope some knight in shining armor sweeps her off her feet and she don't ever think about going back."

"You know there ain't no such thing as no knight," Grace said. "Not today."

"You're right about that."

"That Dr. Gabrielle sure was good looking."

"So is the devil before he shows himself."

"I saw Milton Boykins the other day. You know he sold that old gas station and car wash. They're going to tear it down and build a new drug store."

"We need another drug store like we need a hole in the head. This town ain't big enough for all of that. How much did he get for it?"

"Now, that I don't know. If I can't afford it then I don't ask. But he got enough to buy him a house out on the beach and take that wife of his on a cruise."

"I ain't nothing 'bout no dern cruise boat. I read about all them people getting sick. He should be seeing after his boy Monty. He should've been busy keeping that son of his away from my Thandy. That boy ain't never getting out of jail. All the money in the world can't replace the rod. He should've whipped his behind the first time he got caught drinking out there on 6th Street."

Grace frowned, but Yvetta kept going.

"They gave him life with no parole and he deserves every day of it. That Boykins would have done good to keep that boy away from Thandy."

"How long are you going to blame him for that?"

"Until they put him in the ground and throw dirt on his casket. Thandy got it in her to get out there with them. I don't mind telling you that Simon took a strap to her behind."

Grace was silent. Yvetta went on.

"She deserved every lick. I ain't never had to worry about my Vonnie straying the path like that. But that Thandywaye, she did what she dern well pleased. But, I told her not in this house. Not here."

The Jesus hanging over the Zenith seemed to be frowning, too.

"That Bible of yours tells us to forgive one another. Don't you have enough room in your heart for that? Besides, Thandy seems to be making her own way."

"The Bible tells us not to be fools, Grace. To put on the full armor of God. That includes the Belt of Truth. If I ain't said it once, I have said it a thousand times. I got plenty of forgiveness. But, I ain't no dern laundry mat. I ain't got same day service."

"Even the dry cleaners don't take more than a week."

"See after what's yours," Yvetta shot back.

"Mercy me." Grace was immediately disappointed. She finished the last spot of her coffee and left.

Yvetta closed and latched the screen door behind her. The gray metal frame shook. She had a stack of mostly unopened letters from Thandy somewhere deep in her closet. Every so often,

Thandy wrote home to tell her parents about the wonderful new life her husband made for them. She had finished high school in Atlanta and enrolled in classes at Georgia State. She dutifully sent pictures of the baby to her mother. Her letters went unanswered. The embossed invitation to Thandy's law school graduation went unopened. She had been home only once when Yvonne called with news that their father had suffered a heart attack. She'd brought Jack with her.

Yvetta shuffled into her bedroom and briefly hunted around for the box of letters. She didn't find it immediately. *Some things are better left where they are*, she told herself, shutting the closet door.

The phone was ringing again. She ignored it and went back out to the porch. It was well after eight o'clock in the evening. Nobody would be ringing her line with good news and she didn't have the stomach for anything bad.

Chapter 8

The storm hit just as the sun docked over the city. The September sky was gray and thunder clapped in the distance as the warm rain fell. The street below was barely visible through the dense, lingering fog. Etienne sat alone in the large, wood-paneled conference room, sipping a vanilla latte. She watched the rain fall against the large window, suddenly uneasy with her decision. Wynn Finlayson was stuck in court a few blocks away and decidedly late for his three o'clock appointment. She tapped her watch and settled in further. The rain was coming down in thick white sheets now. For a moment, she wanted to give in, to go home and start again.

She glanced at her watch. The Patek Philippe that adorned her wrist had been a Christmas gift from Jack. The Golden Eclipse had cost more than ten thousand dollars. She unsnapped the clasp and stared at the inscription on back of the face. *"For now and always"* it read. *"12/25/97."*

There had been good years, she admitted to herself. And she wanted another Christmas morning with the boys, another holiday in Telluride watching Jack zoom down the slopes. She wanted for summers on Sea Island, evenings when she would sit between his knees and read from a shared novel while their sons played on the private stretch of beach. She wanted to listen to him quote Shakespeare in Spanish.

But more than anything else, she wanted for the days when he would stroke her hair with his long narrow fingers and remind her that he was hers. Jack adored what he called long "blow" hair. Etienne now regretted cutting hers. It never grew back longer than the base of her neck and he took the haircut as a slap in the face.

She missed her life, their life. It had been long noticed that the Gabrielles no longer appeared together at various charitable functions.

The once coveted invitation to the annual Swan Ball was soundly ignored. It had been years since they enjoyed a concert from a center orchestra table at the Chastain Amphitheatre or even took a decent vacation. The annual two-week stay on Sea Island had been pared down to four insufferable days. Jack and Etienne put on a charade of bliss to shield their sons from the disappointment. With this charade came obligatory sex. That's what she called it these days.

It started with some medical conference years ago. Etienne knew that Jack and Thandy had secretly boarded separate planes for Los Angeles. They checked into the Beverly Hilton under assumed names. Etienne took account of the tryst and hurled an increasing mountain of accusations. She threw around words like shame and humiliation as she conveniently placed her own lengthy string of misdeeds into a neatly packed compartment of mitigating factors. Jack accused her of caring more about what good people thought than the state of the union. Divorce was served with breakfast each morning. The evening nightcap was peppered with further threats. All of which Jack seemed to summarily ignore. For a while, he didn't come home until midnight, then 2:00 a.m., then 4:00. These days she was lucky if he showed his face by noon the next day.

Etienne could not decide whether sleeping alone was better than sleeping with a man who did not love her. Leaving now was as good of a time as any. She absentmindedly took a sip of coffee; it was cold. There in the palatial offices of Hilderbrant, Finlayson, and Moss, her always was coming to an end.

Wynn Finlayson arrived in the office flustered. He quickly composed himself and gave her a strong hug. The attorney had been a good friend over the years, a good person to call on such short notice. Wynn and Liddy Finlayson, one of only a few white couples with whom they had close relations, had often used the summerhouse and Liddy had been a fellow board member with the Junior League. In the early years, the women volunteered together, hosting fundraisers for one worthy cause or another. The men, Wynn and Jack, took off on a once a year "boys only" holiday, sometimes ice fishing in Alaska, sometimes white dove hunting in Mexico or skiing in Telluride. For a couple of years straight, the dynamic duo went down to Brazil to celebrate Carnivale and watch the pretty brown girls in spaghetti thongs. Mancations, they called them.

Etienne would not cry over what was lost, she told herself, but rather she would try to focus on what was before her. Life without Jack would be different. If it would be better, she could not say. Etienne had not allowed herself to imagine it.

At that moment, she wanted it all to be over. No drawn out, traumatic trial, no property dispute. Just over. At five hundred dollars an hour, Finlayson was among the best good money could buy. He read through the paperwork, carefully giving counsel about the various legal issues. She scanned the boxes on the first page and checked the one next to "irreconcilable differences."

She would get half of everything, Finlayson advised. There would be nothing left for the presumed brood of whores Jack kept company with. If he put up a fight, she would add adultery, mental abuse, and abandonment to the filing, soiling the public reputation he so enjoyed.

"We have to list a date of separation," Finlayson advised.

"But we still live in the same house."

"When did you last have sex?"

"What?"

"Legally," Finlayson patiently explained, "that is your separation date."

Etienne thought hard. "New Year's Eve," she said softly.

"Nine months ago?"

"No, last year. Twenty-one months. I suppose he was afraid I would get pregnant."

Wynn had already heard the story of Etienne's well-timed pregnancies from Jack. He also knew how she'd used the boys as anchors when the union teetered on rough seas.

"I know he's hiding money somewhere. Can we find it?"

"Are you sure?"

"Yes, I know he is."

"He's my friend, Etienne. As are you," he advised. "But if the son of a bitch is hiding assets, I will find them. You're my client."

After the brief meeting, the soon-to-be former Mrs. Etienne Renee Pulliam Gabrielle paid the handsome retainer and signed the formal petition for divorce. Finlayson loaned her an umbrella, just in case the rain picked up again, then walked her to the elevator. She got into a waiting car and went directly to Hartsfield-Jackson International where she boarded a shuttle flight to the District. Bleary eyed, overwhelmed, and stewing in grief, she ordered a vodka and tonic to numb the storm raging in her head, to quell the war in her spirit. She longed for the one place where she had been endlessly adored, fawned upon, and loved beyond measure. Another waiting town car ferried her through Washington on her passage to her childhood home.

Georgetown, which borders the Potomac, had been a burgeoning industrial hub at the turn of the century. Flour mills and wharves were plentiful. Prosperity had flowed like sweet honey. While in the beginning tobacco had been the lifeblood of the city, commercial shipping soon erupted from the port, spilling the resulting wealth to all who came. The economic boom drew freed slaves who migrated to the area in droves, many of whom were experienced tobacco processors, hailing from plantations in Virginia and North Carolina. By the late 1950s, when the Pulliam family settled there, the quarter was again fully alive with commerce. Hip coffeehouses and tea rooms sprang from the shadows. Crumbling turn-of-the-century buildings were transformed into art galleries and haute couture boutiques.

Situated just off the square, the Pulliam townhouse is graciously furnished and boasts an expansive kitchen with a coveted butler's pantry. There are three overly large bedrooms, connected by narrow hallways, gentle reminders of the day in which the home was built. The interior is filled with well-kept pieces that had been picked up along the family's travels abroad. Bought for a mere pittance on Bishop Pulliam's then meager salary, the furnishings are now collectively worth more than the home itself. The brownstone had been purchased by the church for the bishop's use while in office and gifted to him upon his retirement from the Baltimore-Washington United Methodist Conference.

Prior to his final assignment, Bishop Jean-Paul Pulliam served two districts with distinction, in Boston and Pittsburgh, before moving to Georgetown. In 1954, he took an extended sabbatical in France, where he met Helene Louise de Campis, a lay worker in the church. Years later, the couple married. A short time later, Etienne Renee was born in the countryside just outside of Rouen, located a hundred or so miles northwesterly of Paris. The Pulliams moved into a spacious cottage just off Rue de Campulley. The family returned stateside two years later to rejoin the Baltimore-Washington conference where the bishop was installed. All told, he remained in service of the church for more than fifty years, which represented the entirety of his adult life.

He preached less frequently in his later years, giving only periodic sermons to host congregations across the district. Helene and Etienne joined him on most occasions. From the pulpit, he trumpeted the grace and mercy of Christ. God's pleasure for those who lived in keeping with His will, to those who prayed without ceasing. He preferred to lay out the facts of the matter with simplicity in a methodical, instructive tone, as opposed to using flowery emotive language. As a child, Etienne would always become bored and fall asleep on the front pew.

As she sat in her lawyer's office, weighing the matter of her imminent divorce, Etienne's father's signature sermon replayed itself. As the plane descended, she could hear his deep baritone voice. She could almost see him standing proudly dressed in the long black robe.

"By His very nature, the Lord is relational," he sounded from the podium, waving his thick hands over the crowd. "He delights in us when we treat one another well, when we live faithful, orderly lives. We glorify Him when we honor the bounds of marriage with our fidelity, when we keep our promises to our children and hold fast to His unchanging hand. The Good Book tells us even that it is unpleasant to Him when we quarrel with our brothers, that our disagreements should be settled on the way to the courthouse."

The congregation clapped. Sparse, though politely fervent "amens" came from the gallery. Etienne yawned. She'd heard the same sermon at least a dozen times before at other churches on other Sundays. At least she heard enough pieces to recognize it as the same. She always woke just as the benediction was recited. Never prone to ardent scolding, the bishop was usually silent on the ride home. He'd utter a few curt phrases in French and that would be the end of it. "The frozen chosen," Etienne would come to call the flock. She worshiped no God more fully than herself.

In 1973, Etienne was enrolled in the Washington Girls' Day kindergarten a few blocks away on Davenport Street. Housed on two separate five-acre campuses in northwest Washington, D.C., the institution was founded by Mary Alice Chandler, a "creative, vibrant spirit" and daughter of a Presbyterian minister, who had been previously a teacher in a missionary school in India. A close associate and confidante of Eleanor Roosevelt, Headmaster Chandler held her position from the school's opening in 1946 until her retirement in 1992. She took a special fondness for Etienne, who was diligent in her studies and readily shared pictures and stories from her family's travels with her classmates. Under Chandler's tutelage, Etienne flourished both academically and socially, despite not infrequent stares from the white students. In

1986, during her senior year, Etienne was elected to the prestigious Council of Students, an honor reserved for the intellectual elite. The headmaster pressed young Etienne to seek a career in the Foreign Service, given her knack for languages. Much to Chandler's displeasure, the affable young woman had her mind on one thing—finding a suitable husband, one who could keep her in the style to which she was accustomed.

Helene busied herself with mothering of her daughter, her Tuesday bridge club, lay work in the church, and frequent lunches with other housewives. When the Spelman acceptance letter arrived, the Pulliams saw their only daughter off for the last time. She would not return for more than a weekend at a time, preferring to spend her summers abroad. Five years later, in 1991, the Pulliams traveled to Atlanta to witness and officiate her wedding to Dr. Jackson Leland Gabrielle.

Etienne fought her way through the terminal traffic, found the waiting town car, and settled into the backseat for the ride home.

Chapter 9

Helene Pulliam welcomed her only child with open arms. Despite her monumental reputation for impassioned, if not histrionic, tirades, Etienne settled into her parents' townhouse without fanfare. Had she announced her arrival, preparations might have been made, but she didn't want to put her mother through the trouble of finding fresh sheets or worrying over how she might take her eggs.

Etienne sought refuge in a second floor guestroom that doubled as the late bishop's study. It had been her bedroom, though little evidence of that remained. The lace bedspreads and sheer white curtains were gone. Her dolls and high school yearbooks had been packed up and stored in the basement. Mementos from Bishop Pulliam's travels and work now crowded the wall-length bookshelf, including his purple cleric's collar and the shawl he wore to the installation ceremony. Her mother's sewing basket, covered in unfinished knit work, sat in a far corner, obviously unused for several years. There was little room to store her suitcases. She abandoned them, unpacked, in the middle of the floor.

Etienne hunkered down in the cluttered bedroom/study for days on end. She emerged only to eat or relieve herself, both of which she did little. She disregarded the Bible that her mother left on the nightstand. Helene left it open to the Book of Job. It was a gentle invitation, and one soundly ignored. She emerged on day six with matted hair and an unpleasant stench. At her mother's urging, Etienne drew a bath, put on fresh clothes, and joined her for lunch at the Potomac Club. "The bed will draw your strength," Helene advised, her French accent still strong.

Etienne sat on her mother's vanity stool, wearing only a bath towel, brushing the tangles from her hair as she watched Helene steam press a crumbled Dolce & Gabbana daisy jacquard dress drawn from the suitcase.

"There," Helene said as she finished. "You will be at least presentable."

Etienne washed her face in the basin, then disappeared down the hallway. Helene retrieved the car.

Splendid oils of the club's founding members adorned the walls of the imposing reception hall. They were serious men like the room that welcomed its visitors. Tall slender women in black A-line dresses greeted them from behind a solid wood podium. No reservation had been needed given the bishop's prior position on the club's board of governors. His name was among those etched on a plaque that hung above the hostess stand.

"Mrs. Pulliam, it's a pleasure to have you with us," a young hostess greeted. Despite the busy lunch crowd, she gave a knowing glance to another who spirited off to clear an appropriate table. Someone would have to be hurried along in order to make way for the Pulliams. Helene, a woman of pedestrian taste, did not care for such fuss, but her husband's position demanded it. When shown to the table, she gave an approving nod.

The inside of the Potomac Club looked like every other private dining room in the District. Heavy crown moldings, mahogany wood finishes, marble flooring, extravagant chandeliers, and tables draped in white, pressed cloths. Waiters and busmen in short white waistcoats scurried about the room, ferrying thick prime rib sandwiches, lentil soups, and blackened chicken Caesar salads. It was just past twelve-thirty when they arrived and most of the tables were full. A dining room attendant appeared immediately and poured two glasses of sparkling water.

Ignoring the bustling room, Helene smiled graciously at the attendant, took a sip from the cool sweating glass, and said, "I'm worried about you."

"I know, but you shouldn't be. People get divorced every day. I should have left sooner."

"Have you at least called Jackson?"

"No. If he has something to say now then he should say it to my lawyer. That's what I pay Finny for."

"He's called several times."

Helene Pulliam was not a good liar. She aimed her clear blue eyes at the white tablecloth to hide the deception. The truth of the matter is that Jack had called only once to inquire about his wife's well-being. Helene thought it better to tell her daughter otherwise.

A waiter stopped by and rambled off a list of memorized appetizers and the day's specials. "The lobster ravioli is a special treat," he advised. "As are the crab cake sandwiches."

"We'll have them," Etienne said, shooing him away, ignoring whatever her mother might have preferred. "And a fruit plate."

He hadn't gotten two feet away before she waved him back.

"A bottle of your best merlot, please."

"Domestic?"

"Of course."

"We have a fine Duckhorn Vineyard, 1994."

Etienne nodded. The waiter set off anew.

"Etienne, you know I don't drink."

"If you did, Mother, then we'd need two."

As if reading her daughter's thoughts, Helene paused and said, "Honey, a divorce is a traumatic experience. You don't have to pretend for me."

Etienne was immediately ashamed of the bottle of wine. When the waiter brought it to the table and presented it for inspection, Etienne abruptly told him to take it away.

"We'll have two sweet iced teas if you have it," she said looking away. "And lemon please."

After presenting the drinks, the waiter returned with Maryland crab cake sandwiches, the special appetizer, and a plate of fresh berries. Etienne picked at the fruit and decided she couldn't stomach a single bite.

"You should eat something," Helene prodded.

"I don't feel like eating."

Helene took a sip of tea. "You haven't said a word about the boys. How are they taking the news?"

"As well as can be expected. They're staying with Gail for a while."

Abigail Stewart, a twenty-year friend and sorority sister from her days at Spelman, readily took the boys for a few days. Etienne hadn't told Jack where they were and Gail had strict orders to call if Jack made an attempt to see Jack and Jacob.

"I'll shoot his black ass if I have to," Gail assured.

Etienne silently wished it would come to that. In her estimation, Jack had been something short of a worthless father.

"The boys are fine, Mother. This is the best thing for them."

"I suppose you're right."

Helene examined her daughter's face.

"Arrogant fool." She was talking in rapid bursts now, quickly making up for six days of tortured silence. "That's what he is. I don't mind telling you, Mother, that he hasn't touched me in well over a year. He wants me to believe that there is no one else. If I am anything at all, I'm not stupid. Lies. I am sick of the lies. He doesn't even have enough respect to come home at night. It's horrible, Mother. Just horrid," she said, twisting the diamond wedding band and engagement ring. "I can't believe I married him."

She got tired of twisting, took off the Harry Winston six-carat diamond wedding set and plopped it into the half glass of tea. Helene raised her left brow and watched it float to the bottom. Resting in the glass, the diamond seemed even larger and more brilliant.

"Where does he say he's been?"

"When he's not on call, and that's every weekend," Etienne explained, "he says he sleeps at the office. Sometimes he doesn't even come home to change clothes. Yet, he mysteriously shows up in a fresh suit."

"It must have been difficult for you," Helene lamented.

"He doesn't even care. I've pleaded and begged. After fifteen years, I've been reduced to begging."

Etienne excused herself from the table and fumbled her way to the ladies' room. She rushed into an open stall and threw up.

After ten minutes, Helene grew concerned. She dumped the tea into an empty water glass, dried off the ring, and put it in her coin purse. She found Etienne hovered over the commode, wet-faced and pitiful.

"Come now dear," she said wrapping her arms around Etienne's shoulders. "Let's get you home."

Helene dabbed Etienne's face with a cool hand-cloth and led her out of the restroom.

The women had just arrived at the townhouse when Etienne's cell phone rang. She sequestered herself in the lower parlor and took the call.

"Are you ready for this?" Finlayson asked. "Jack's attorney has filed a response."

"He isn't contesting the divorce, is he?"

She stretched out on the love seat, kicked off her Jimmy Choo slingbacks, and listened.

"Quite the contrary, he is offering a settlement."

"Premature, don't you think? He doesn't know what I want."

"The offer is more than generous."

"For fifteen years and two sons, it very well should be," she snarled.

"You might be surprised."

"Gimme the number."

"Five million. Based on his known assets, it's more than equitable."

"The hell it is," Etienne said. She swallowed and asked, "What about the house?"

"He contends that it is not marital property since it was a family home before you married him. However, the offer allows for the purchase of a new home of similar value."

"And Sea Island? What about the summerhouse?"

"He's willing to share it. Alternating summers."

"I don't want it anyway. He kept his bitches down there," she sniffed. "And Telluride? What about the chalet?"

"It's yours. The judge might demand mediation."

"How long will it take?"

"Sixty days, maybe. That depends on which judge we draw. I'll shop for the most expedient. And one more thing. Jack wants to know where the boys are. The judge won't like it if you're hiding them."

"They're here with me in Washington," she lied.

Finlayson knew better, but didn't challenge her. "Did you know Jack bought a condo five years ago?" he continued.

She sat straight up and asked, "Where?"

"In Buckhead. Paid cash."

"No."

"I am including it in the filing."

"Who lives there?"

She could hear papers rustling. "Thandywaye Malone. Do you know her?" Finlayson asked.

"Unfortunately." Etienne could barely hold back her venom.

"The property was listed in both her name and Jack's until a month ago. A quit claim deed was filed removing her name from the record."

Etienne dropped her head and her shoulders slumped. Damp-faced, she pulled a Kleenex from a box on the cocktail table. She told Finlayson she would call later. She stepped into the kitchen where her mother was emptying and filling the dishwasher.

"It's almost over, Mother. He wants to get rid of me so badly that he's willing to pay through the nose."

She fell into her mother's waiting arms and began to cry.

"He bought that tramp a house!"

Helene ignored the possibility that Jack wasn't everything the bishop thought him to be.

"We have to get you cleaned up," she consoled.

After another long bath, Etienne steadied herself. She went back to the parlor and phoned Finlayson.

"Tell him I want fifteen million," she demanded. "One for every year. That's over and above the boys' trust funds and monthly support payments. Every penny that state allows. He's got every dime of that and more. Tell him I won't take one red cent less."

Chapter 10

At six in the evening, the first streaks of dusk painted the sky as the trail along Lake Michigan began to empty. Thandy glanced over the horizon where the blue waters met the purple-stained sky. She let her eyes wander over the limestone-encrusted beach to trace the divide. Somewhere beyond it lay the world, the life she left behind, the end of a chapter.

She could feel her breasts bobbing; the soles of her feet burned; sweat poured down the center of her back; her chest pounded. She cursed every hill up and down as she crossed through Promontory Point, past the aquarium and beyond. Still she ran. A group of chatty power walkers lingered somewhere behind her. She had been amused with their henhousing, the doings of their husbands, a neighbor's philandering ways. Others had come on ten speed bikes and still others floated by on rollerblades. One after the other zoomed by and she let them.

"Run your own race," Thandy told herself.

Mr. Blue Shorts was fifty yards or better up ahead. She marveled at his taut leg muscles and how they expanded with his stride. She'd stolen a look at his bare broad chest as he passed. His skin was rich and smooth like chocolate cake batter—the kind your mother would let you lick right out of the bowl. She slowed to a manageable shuffle, admiring his backside as it disappeared up and over a bridge. That was good, too. It was almost a relief to see something wonderful, something that didn't immediately remind her of Jack. She kept running. Chocolate cake never looked so good in blue shorts!

If she made it back to Hyde Park, she'd force herself to do a hundred crunches, she promised. Liposuction wasn't an option. She had another three miles of trail left, give or take, and then at least two more on the street. The trail ended in a park. She cut across the green, through a parking lot, and over Hyde Park Boulevard, where the traffic was heavy. A white Chevy barreled through the light, barely missing her. The driver blew his horn.

She shook it off and ran on. She'd been in Chicago just under a month. It had been just under two since she'd last seen Jack. Forty-five days, four hours, and fifteen minutes to be exact. She'd managed to avoid him until she and Montana boarded the plane. She would learn, she told herself, to stop counting the breaths, to stop walking between the raindrops. She moved swiftly through the business district, passing a stone church and a row of assorted eateries and barbershops. Memories of her life with Jack came with every stride. She remembered every detail. All ten years' worth. She was too worn out to get angry again. Too tired to be mad. Too full of resolve to go back. *Keep going.*

She owed something to herself, but she wasn't sure what. She just didn't want to be last in line anymore. Thandy picked up the pace again as she passed a line of brick row houses and century old tenements, almost racing by the school yard as she made the last turn onto her block. She gave it a final kick as she entered from the paved alleyway. Her neighbors to the left and right were a gingerly mix of doctors, professors, and assorted other professionals: some white, most black, some of whom worked for the University of Chicago in one capacity or another. It was a good place for her daughter, she reasoned. Someplace she would encounter people from varied walks of life, with circumstances dif-

ferent from their own. She wanted Montana to appreciate their
life, the early years that Thandy hadn't yet found the words to tell
her about.

Montana was sitting on the sofa eating chips and a diet cola
when Thandy stumbled into the door.

"Hey, kiddo," she blew out.

"I was about to send out a search party. You want some dinner?" Montana said, clicking down the TV volume.

Thandy hadn't thought about food. Just chocolate cake.

"I'm good. Not really hungry."

"How far did you run?"

"Oh, just down Lake Michigan to downtown and back."

"And back?"

"Yeah."

"Mom, that's gotta be twenty miles."

"Twenty-two," she huffed. "I had a little encouragement."

"You're not a *serious* runner, you know?"

"Yeah, well, I am now. I was following this guy who had a
good pace going."

"You mean he was good looking."

"Watch yourself, young lady," Thandy warned in a motherly
tone.

"O.K. so he *was* fine. That made you run twenty-two miles?"

"No. He just livened up the scenery," she giggled.

Montana thought for a moment, then said, "It's okay if you
date, you know."

"And I need whose permission?"

"I'm just saying . . . well, maybe I should run you a cold
bath."

"That won't be necessary," she laughed. "I can hold it together."

Thandy dragged herself through the dining room and disappeared into the kitchen. Montana eased off the sofa and followed.
Thandy stumbled past a refrigerator full of bottled water and
stuck her mouth under the sink faucet. She let the coolness run
all over her face.

Montana stood arms crossed in the archway. At seventeen, she already had a beautifully sculpted figure and a serious, though somewhat easy disposition. She was her mother's self-appointed protector.

"Are you going to drown yourself now?"

"Not a chance. I can think of better ways to die than that. Hand me a towel."

Montana tossed her a dry towel.

"Drowning? Now that would be too easy," Thandy said, shaking away the water. "Besides, I ain't got time to die."

They were still laughing when Thandy felt a dull pain radiating in her lower back.

"Are you all right?"

"Yeah, baby. I'm okay."

"Maybe you're running too much."

Thandy pulled her head out of the sink and looked at her daughter. She admired her grace. Truly a force of nature, Montana had been blessed with her father's face. It was perfectly symmetrical, almost better than perfect. At five-foot-eight, she was a full six inches taller than her mother—another gift from her father. Save for the electric coral-colored eyes and an ironclad will, she inherited almost nothing from Thandy. She watched Montana stand over the kitchen island studying a stack of mail, and picking through a magazine. *You're so much better than me, so much smarter. Don't you dare fall for some slick-talking bastard. It'll wreck everything. Everything I gave you.*

In the month since they arrived in Chicago, Thandy had run almost every day. Never prone to invite her daughter into her troubles, she was satisfied that Montana remained puzzled about the sudden move. Thandy never talked about men, least of all the very married Jack Gabrielle. If Montana believed her mother to be a monk, Thandy thought it would be just fine. As she matured, it had been increasingly difficult to hide him, to mask her glee whenever he did something wonderful, or to bury the pain when he didn't.

"If you're going to run like that, you'll need better shoes," Montana chided. "A heart monitor wouldn't hurt."

There she was, already talking like a doctor. In a few months, she would head to Connecticut for undergraduate studies at Yale, where she planned to major in biology.

Thandy was certain, if not wishful, that her daughter was still a virgin. *You would tell me, right? Maybe I shouldn't have bought you such a nice car.*

"Did you finish unpacking your room?"

"Of course I did."

"Thank you."

"For what?"

"For giving me a few less things to worry about."

Thandy knew the answer before she asked. Montana was an orderly creature. *Your room is clean. Now, just tell me you haven't had sex,* she pleaded in her head. Montana was far too beautiful to go unnoticed. Thandy opened her arms and wrapped herself around her. She had been a good mother, she tried to tell herself. Montana was living proof that her sacrifices were paying off.

"I love you, Mommy."

"Thank you, baby," Thandy returned. "I love you, too."

After a cold supper, Thandy forgot her crunches, popped in a movie, and settled down on the sofa. Montana sat on the floor between her mother's legs. Thandy parted her daughter's hair in neat sections and slicked oil on her scalp. Montana closed her eyes and let her mind float off to nowhere.

Thandy began braiding her hair in perfect rows from the front to the nape of her neck, gently twisting and pulling the strands into order. The long cornrows fell generously below Montana's shoulder blades. Thandy began to hum. Her voice was low and deep, soothing and soulful. Soon Montana was humming, too.

Both were sounding drowsy, wrapped up in each other's arms, before the movie was finished. Montana's hip pressed against her mother's thigh; their heartbeats in close sync. While most girls her age were declaring their independence, pushing the edge of the envelope, Montana was still her mother's child. Thandy gazed at her face as she slept, taking her in, all at once admiring and prideful.

She was alone now and that was fine. Leaving Jack was so much easier than being gone, she kept saying to herself. She'd folded her tent, closed camp, and set off for something new. Maybe she was weak for running away, but she didn't want to bump into him on the street and pretend there had been nothing.

Chapter 11

After eight hours of sporadic sleep, Thandy rose before dawn and readied herself for her first day of work. Montana was already awake, bright eyed and bushy tailed, searching her closet for the right outfit to wear to school.

"Mom, whaduya think?"

"Hmmm, I don't think pink is your color."

"It was my color last year."

"Honey, it's fall. And isn't that my shirt?"

"Argh!"

"You asked."

"I guess you're right."

"I always am. Now put my shirt back where you found it. It's too small for you anyway."

Twenty minutes later, Thandy watched as Montana backed her car out of the detached, two-car garage just as the lawn sprinklers got going for the morning. A cautious person by nature, Montana was almost as reliable as the automated system. Thandy watched her pull into the alleyway and onto the street.

Thandy nursed her second thermos of coffee that morning as she drove along through the rush hour. The traffic inched along slowly, but steadily. She beat back the uneasy feeling that crept up in her stomach. She'd been a little queasy that morning, but quickly chalked it up to nerves. Her thigh muscles twitched and jumped. Her back still ached a little. Maybe a little less caffeine, she reasoned. She was too young for a heart monitor, but a better pair of running shoes wasn't such a bad idea.

She fumbled her way to Madison Street and parked her car in the underground lot. The space on the first level already had her name on it. She looked at the painted sign that read "Reserved 24 hours, Campbell-Perkins President" and smiled slightly. She grabbed her briefcase and unloaded a box from the trunk. A passerby offered a hand, but Thandy declined.

On the way up, the elevator stopped on the fourth and eighteenth floors. Four men and a woman got on at the fourth floor. All were nicely tailored. Thandy's eyes panned first to the Brooks Brothers' shoes, then upward to their white faces. A black girl, no more than twenty-five, got on at eighteen. Her Payless pumps and thin, flowery skirt said she was at best somebody's secretary. Thandy smiled warmly and said good morning. The girl said nothing at first. She returned a polite smile when she realized Thandy was talking to her. Everyone else in the elevator, all the white faces, spoke only to one another, consumed in serious conversation. Thandy shifted the box in her arms, got a better grip on her briefcase, tipped her head, and got off on the forty-second floor.

The office was larger than she had imagined. The executive suite was luxuriously furnished with a collection of tufted leather chairs, polished wood, and artwork. The smoked-glass wall behind the empty reception desk was emblazoned with the Campbell-Perkins logo. It was 7:30 a.m. and the phones were already ringing. The place was alive with associates hauling coffee and bagels. Several meetings were already underway. No less than six secretaries, already perched behind their desks, answered the buzzing phones with warm "good mornings."

No one noticed her at first. Thandy looked around, searching for a place to put down the box she'd hauled up from the car. A tall slender woman greeted her.

"Good morning. How can I help you?"

"I'm Thandywaye Malone."

The woman was at first confused, then overly kind. "Ms. Malone?" she said taking the box. "I'm sorry, I . . ."

"It's okay. Good morning."

"It's good to finally meet you. I'm Susan DeGross, Director of Operations."

"Good to meet you, Ms. DeGross." Thandy guessed she was another overblown office manager.

"The driver didn't help you with this?"

"What driver?"

"How did you get here?"

"I drove."

Susan smiled. "Your driver is probably still waiting outside your house."

"I have a driver?" she asked, understanding the corporate culture immediately.

"Yes, ma'am. Every member of the executive team has a driver. Mr. Thomas will come every morning at 7:00 or any time that you prefer. He'll be on call throughout the day and take you home each evening. Your office is ready."

Thandy followed her down the lengthy stretch of hallway. John Stafford, a senior vice president and the chief investment officer, met them. Stafford was a fifty-something, short, brick of a man who ambled along as gracefully as a sack of potatoes. He interviewed her twice, the first time at a restaurant on Navy Pier.

Riva's central dining room had a breathtaking view of the Chicago skyline and Lake Michigan. Thandy selected a filet mignon, partly because the server had been so enthusiastic about its quality, but mostly because it would not have been Jack's preference. She hadn't enjoyed a piece of beef in ten years. Liberation had begun.

"Thandywaye! Top of the morning to you!" he boomed in a heavy Irish accent as he greeted her in the hallway.

She nodded and smiled, "Thandy is just fine."

"It's an interesting name. I never asked you about the history." He walked with her to her office.

"It was my father's middle name. Simon Thandywaye Mbeki.

His family emigrated from South Africa in the 1950s and changed their surname to Malone. It was one thing to be colored, but quite another to be straight off the boat from Africa," she laughed.

Her father, the strict disciplinarian, brought his traditional African values with him to the United States. Spare the rod and spoil the child, he believed. Simon Mbeki also believed that a man should earn his own way. Accepting a job referral from his wife's father meant he would have to work twice as hard to prove himself. He would lead an orderly life, one beyond reproach. Even though he had shed his African surname, there were some things he would not leave behind. Thandy knew her defiance had been heartbreaking. He had blamed her destruction on the evils of American media, the disrespectful music, and readily available drugs. He didn't live to see the string of victories she could now count up and Thandy regretted never being a source of pride. She wished her father could see her now. She hoped he would be pleased.

"It's good to have you, Thandywaye," said Stafford.

"It's good to be here."

During the interview at Riva's, Stafford had been coy at first, but then direct in his questioning. "Where did you go to school? Why law? What are you like under pressure? Does your team like or respect you? Why? You're thirty-four. Why do you think you're ready to run a multibillion dollar business? Why would our clients trust you with their money?"

She answered him straightaway. "Emory. My grandfather said I'd make a great lawyer. I'm cool. And I'm sure they respect me. But liking me is another question and irrelevant I might add. I'm a tough administrator and tough on details. I am selective about my words and concise in my instruction. And you called me. I'm sure you knew my age, birth weight, and shoe size before the headhunter picked up the phone. My track record alone commands the trust of your client base."

Thandy didn't flinch. If nothing else, she had inherited her father's unflappable bearings. Living in Simon's house had been a trial by fire. Ironically, even as he wielded the leather strap, he had taught her how to fight, how to endure pain. She had come a long way from Winston-Salem. The difference now is that she had a daughter of her own. She wanted better for Montana. Stafford was immediately impressed, but kept up the game. He fired another round of queries. Again, she answered quickly, leaving little room for doubt. After the first hour, he gave in. His expression softened. He leaned in casually and told her how impressed the team had been with her credentials.

"You managed to accomplish a great deal in a short period of time."

She watched Stafford's thick white hands as he mapped out the inner workings of Perkins-Campbell on the back of a bar napkin. Privately held, the firm houses four units and eight thousand employees inhabit sixty offices around the world. With eighty billion under management, they were giving the big boys a run for their money. The mother ship is located at First National Plaza in Chicago. The founding partners, Jerry Perkins and Peter Lloyd Campbell, started out with a small savings and loan in Naperville, a town that sits just west of Chicago, fifty years ago. Jerry Perkins, Jr., the elder son of one of the founders, was chairman, president, and CEO until last year when he handed the reins to his younger brother. Young, quick-tempered, and driven, Joel Perkins fired three division presidents his first day on the job. Two new division presidents were promoted from within the ranks. He wanted stronger talent for the Wealth Management practice. The board agreed with him. Perkins also created a new chief operating officer's job to oversee the division chiefs. Résumés flowed in from around the country.

"There's a second search underway," Stafford explained further. "We haven't found the right fit. It could take a year or better; we're in no rush."

"I'm certain they will find the right talent."

"If I have any say in the matter, you'll be our next president in Wealth Management. But that's up to Mr. Perkins and the board."

"I appreciate your confidence."

A week later she returned to Chicago to meet Joel Perkins. The discussion was brief. He knew everything about her, he assured. He leaned back in his chair, admiring his pick like she'd just hit a jump shot from center court at the buzzer. She was everything he was looking for. Thandy had been immediately taken with Joel's sheer mental fortitude, his firm grasp on the normally elusive, and his ability to draw connections to seemingly disparate topics and issues.

The board vote would be unanimous. The compensation committee quickly decided on a generous, seven-figure package. The press release had already been written. Thandywaye Mbeki Malone, age thirty-four, would be the first African-American woman to ever head a major division of a Wall Street firm and she would be among the most highly compensated executives on the Street. The firm's chief diversity officer had been especially effusive. Various industry columnists speculated that she would soon be named COO. The story was strategically leaked to *The New York Times* before the press release hit the street.

The headhunter who recruited her had been persistent. "This is strictly confidential. No one will know you are under consideration," he promised at the time. "If it's not a good fit, you can just walk away and pretend it never happened."

She had promised herself then that it was just a dry run, she was just keeping her options open. She wouldn't accept the job, if offered. She wouldn't leave Atlanta. She wouldn't leave Jack. The offer was barely seventy-two hours old when Etienne called.

"He's where?"

"In Barbados."

"With who?"

"An Angel Delafuenta. But, of course, she's using his last name. That cheap bastard made the conference organizers pay for her plane ticket."

"And you want me to believe that? Where did you get my phone number?" It was the first time she had ever spoken to Mrs. Jack Gabrielle.

"From his cellular bill, of course. You don't have to believe me. I'm just trying to help you."

"Why would you want to do that?"

"Listen, sweetheart, you don't want my husband or you wouldn't be settling for second place, and it's clear he doesn't want you. He loves only himself. That and his bank account."

Thandy hung up, took a deep breath, dialed *69 and called her back.

"Where did you say he was staying?"

"I didn't."

Thandy paced the hardwood floors as she talked.

"When's he due back?"

"Sunday night."

There was silence.

"Ms. Malone, how long have you been seeing my husband?"

"Almost ten years," she returned.

The silence was deafening. Thandy was immediately ashamed. She didn't know how long Etienne had known of their affair. She politely said good-bye and hung up again. She thought about killing the sorry bastard and even went as far as to count the paces he would take from his car to the garage elevator at his office. The first shot would hit him in the ass. She would empty the next five rounds into his head.

But, she'd gone in with eyes open wide. She felt foolish about that now. She had been hoodwinked, bamboozled, and deceived by The Great Jack Gabrielle. Suddenly, she felt herself choking. She told herself Jack wasn't worth a lifetime in jail, that he wasn't worth her sanity. But leaving was easier than being gone. In the end, she took the job in Chicago, packed up her daughter, and left.

We've all got our cross to bear, she told herself as she followed her self-appointed tour guide to the last office on the left. *Stop trying to dodge the raindrops and get yourself an umbrella.*

Susan unlocked the door and waved her arm across the threshold. Stafford followed.

"I took the liberty of ordering some office supplies. The technician will be along shortly with your laptop and BlackBerry," Susan said.

The office manager drew the blinds, revealing a near panoramic view of downtown. The lake was off in the distance. The water was blue, like somebody dropped food coloring in it to pretty things up. She could vaguely make out the trail of redemption. Her feet hurt just thinking about it. Thandy imagined Mr. Blue Shorts making his way over the hills. Chicago had its charms. Her best girlfriend, Phillipa, always called it "Boy Central."

"Beginning at 9:30, we've arranged several interviews for you," Susan announced, as if their roles were reversed.

"Interviews? With whom?"

"Candidates for your support team. I took the liberty of setting up six appointments: three this morning and three this afternoon," Susan said. "They are all highly qualified, but I will arrange for you to see more if necessary. You are budgeted for two."

"You'll need them both," Stafford advised. "A third if you can get it," he winked.

Susan wasn't amused. "We've scheduled lunch with your immediate team at noon," Susan advised. "La Rosetta is on the first floor. They've got great pasta."

Susan kept talking. Stafford looked to Thandy and shrugged his shoulders.

Chapter 12

By late afternoon, Thandy had lunched with her full senior team, met with three junior associates whose only job was to see after her needs, reviewed top-line quarterly financials, picked two secretaries—including the young woman she met briefly on the elevator that morning—and dismissed her driver. By four o'clock she was alone.

She remembered the days when things weren't so good. She certainly didn't have a secretary, let alone two. Then, she didn't have twenty-five hundred employees. Back then there were times when she got by on four hundred dollars a month in welfare and food stamps. Back then was only fifteen years ago. There was no Susan DeGross and nobody cared if she wiped her ass good back then, let alone where or if she had lunch. Then too, she vaguely remembered the long stretch of placidity, the days when she had loved and had been loved.

There had been a nice house, a couple new cars in the garage, and she never had to worry about the light bill. Contrary to what her mother might have wished, Monty had been good to her. He quickly saved up enough money for a down payment on a car wash. Within a year, he owned two more. He purchased a comfortable, spacious house in a new subdivision in South Fulton.

The new business floundered almost immediately, but the money kept rolling in due mostly to Monty's unfortunate agreement with a drug dealer to run dirty cash. Within a year, he bought three more car washes, bringing the total to six. Monty became known as Big Boy on the street, the go-to man for drug peddlers who needed to wash their money and their tricked-out cars.

He bought Thandy a shiny new BMW, equipped with a premium sound system and chrome wheels. He built an even bigger house with a circular drive lined with a stable of other expensive cars. Thandy got her hair done every Friday at a swanky Buckhead salon and sent Montana to a private preschool she saw advertised in a magazine. She didn't think twice about the money and never asked where it came from. As long as the tuition was paid on time, the preschool administrators never questioned it either.

Thandy was seventeen years old, married, and living a grown woman's life, driving a car and living in a house women twice her age couldn't readily afford. At Monty's urging, she had finished high school and enrolled in college, but had otherwise been a stay-at-home mother. Life was coming together nicely.

Then, the bust came.

Just before 3:00 a.m., May 24, 1992, Thandy heard shouting outside the house. The front door blasted from its frame and the motion detector blared. Monty reached for the 9-mm. pistol he kept tucked under the mattress. An FBI agent, dressed in a navy blue T-shirt and a bulletproof vest, took aim at his head before he could get to it. A team of drug enforcement agents flooded into the house. They went room to room with guns drawn seeking out every occupant. She heard them rummaging through closets upstairs. Others were in the basement. They ordered drug-sniffing dogs to search the closets and vents. Drawers of clothing were emptied onto the beds, the carpets torn from the floor. The once perfect decor was now a mess of overturned furniture and clumps of linen stripped from the beds. Even the refrigerator was emptied.

"Ain't nobody here but me and my baby!" Thandy told them. "Please, ain't nobody here but us!"

She heard Montana crying, but an officer blocked her from getting to the nursery. They had her husband spread out naked on the living room floor. She fought her way forward, kicking and screaming. She watched as an agent helped him put on a robe, then cuffed and led him out the front door toward a waiting squad car. An officer read Thandy her Miranda rights while another comforted then two-and-a-half-year-old Montana. They simultaneously raided eight more houses that morning. All of the safe houses were loaded down with cash and uncut cocaine wrapped in duct tape. Monty's empire came crashing down while he sat in a four-by-four holding cell dressed in Thandy's pink terrycloth housecoat. The judge ordered him remanded without bond and moved to seize control of the car washes.

Monty pleaded innocent to two hundred and twelve counts of drug trafficking, money laundering, and wire and mail fraud. After an extended trial, the jury read convictions on all charges, including two counts of felony murder, and the federal judge sentenced him to three life terms. If the Feds ever let him go, which was unlikely, the state would be waiting for him with another murder conspiracy charge. A snitch was still living and breathing, but he had a sordid tale of how Big Boy ordered a hit on his life for shorting him in a transaction.

Thandy didn't know that Monty. The man she knew wouldn't hurt anybody, let alone some petty thief he didn't know any better than Adam's house cat. Whatever he was, he hid it from his young wife. Monty was convicted and sent to the federal penitentiary just east of downtown Atlanta. A few months later, he was transferred to the federal penitentiary at Marion, Illinois, where he shared a cell with Marco Ciprioni, a well-known Mafia kingpin from New Jersey.

At the crack of dawn one morning, Thandy picked the marshal's lock and crept into her house with an empty pillowcase. She moved cautiously through the kitchen, down a long hallway toward the den. She struggled to move a heavy mahogany desk and rolled back the carpet. She swallowed, slowed her breath, and remembered the combination to the safe. After a couple of attempts, the lock clicked. Inside the box lay several bundles of cash. She was relieved the Feds hadn't discovered it. She quickly stuffed the stacks into the makeshift bag and made her way back to the car parked three blocks away. The next day, she went to the lawyer's office and placed the pile of money on his desk.

"I can't say this will help," he conceded. "I'd be lying if I told you one more penny would make any difference."

"Just tell me that it might."

"There is a slim chance, but we can file a dozen appeals before one will stick."

"Then take it. Take all of it."

The lawyer felt through the bundle.

"There has to be more than a hundred grand here."

"I know."

"Take it and make a life for yourself," the lawyer said. "Start over. You do it right and you can turn this money into a nice future for yourself. A nice life for you and your daughter."

"We don't have a life without my husband," she told him. "Whatever he did, he earned this money."

In the end, the money made no difference. Every appeal was denied. It wasn't long before the house was sold at auction. The car washes had been boarded up and awaited sale. The Feds seized what was left including the small bank account she was living on.

Thandy's life was on fire, burning like a cane field in a high wind. She was broke and out of work. She went hungry most nights, subsisting on black coffee and saltine crackers, and the small rented house she wound up being evicted from was infested with rats. Montana was still in state foster care, sent away the night of the bust.

Thandy spent most of her days searching for a job, never able to turn up anything, too proud to put in an application at the local coffee shop where she used to buy a tall caramel macchiato. Phillipa, who until then had just been the girl in the rented house next door, brought over some poison and traps from the local hardware store. She poured small dishes of water and strategically placed them inside the holes in the floorboards, under the kitchen sink, and in the cupboards.

"What you've got are roof rats," Phillipa explained. "They walk right over the power lines and into the attic. They like screwing and waste no time making a nest for the babies. But this will take care of them. Once they take the bait and drink some water, the poison will activate and tear up their insides."

Thandy was glad to have a friend who was an expert on rodents. Together, the women painted the kitchen chocolate brown and hung a pretty border. Thandy never invited anyone else inside. She was too ashamed. That was then.

She hadn't told the firm about her stint in jail and it didn't come up in the routine background check. In 1994, Monty's lawyer petitioned federal court to expunge her name from the court records, and got it. The drug arrest and the prior probation for minor drug use in North Carolina evaporated into the sealed records of the juvenile court system. The eviction record had been acquired and destroyed by an especially crafty friend who went down to the Fulton County courthouse and paid off a clerk. No reputable firm would hire an executive with a spotty financial history, let alone a conviction for drug running and conspiracy. But that was behind her now. As part of her deal to testify against her husband, details of Thandy's life as Mrs. Monty Boykins were kept out of the newspapers. And the welfare records were cloaked under federal privacy statutes. There was no trace of the life she had led.

Over Susan's objections, Thandy drove herself home. She had been in Chicago only a week before she purchased a 2006 silver Mercedes SL 500, her first and only extravagance, which beat the hell out of the Honda Civic that got repossessed twelve years ago. Enjoying the smooth ride of the car, Thandy remembered the purchase. The gaggle of salesmen had ignored her at first. She calmly reached into her purse and drew out her checkbook. Thandy tapped the Louis Vuitton leather booklet on the hood of the car until one of them noticed.

"Welcome to Mercedes-Benz of Chicago. How can I help you?" he said, extending his hand.

"I want this one. Iridium silver metallic with ash leather interior, seven-speed automatic, AMG sport package."

"If you'll step this way, I'll get an application going."

"Not necessary. I'll be paying cash. And by the way, get me a list of your pre-owned C230s. Two years, twenty thousand miles max, with immaculate service records."

The salesman was immediately ashamed. He disappeared into a corner office and emerged with his sales manager.

"Good morning, Mrs.?"

"Malone. Ms. Thandywaye Malone."

"Welcome, Ms. Malone. If you will give me a moment, I will have a porter pull them both around. I have a certified pre-owned C230 we took on trade yesterday. It's blue."

"The color doesn't matter and I don't need to drive them. How much?"

"With tax, tag and title, that will be . . ."

"I'm not paying the list price," she interrupted, placing her left hand on her hip, shifting her weight. "I want your best number, the one you'd give your mother. Drive out with all the bells and whistles. If you come correct the first time, we'll deal today. If not, well, I understand there are dealerships in Naperville and Hoffman Estates. Am I right?"

The sales manager delivered the vehicles personally.

The next day, Thandy purchased a three-bedroom house in Hyde Park on the corner of Ellis Avenue and 53rd Street. She could well afford one of the sprawling mansions in Naperville and Waukegan, but she had fallen in love with the stone-faced, century-old home. She wanted to live in the center of the city. The house still had its original crown molding, copper wiring, slate roof, and hardwood floors. A two-story penthouse on Lake

Michigan with twelve-foot ceilings was certainly appealing, but she wanted Montana to feel some sense of permanence. Thandy needed it, too.

She was home less than fifteen minutes before she changed into her running shorts, laced her newly acquired Jordan running shoes, and went to stretch on the sidewalk outside the front gate. *Maybe Mr. Blue Shorts is out there tonight.* The thought alone brought a deep broad grin to her face. It was better to fantasize about a man she didn't know than to stew over a decade of bad choices she made with Jack. She took off with a strong stride, quickly covering eight blocks. She dipped through the business district with her ponytail bobbing in the wind. A wave of cramps hit before she made it to Hyde Park Boulevard. At first she pushed on, then gave up when she couldn't take another step. She turned and walked back home. Her legs trembled. Even her fingers were shaking. All she wanted was to make it upstairs to a long, hot shower. She made it as far as the sofa and collapsed.

Chapter 13

Thandy stood in the shower stall weeping. Not for what life had become, but for what it had been. Not for what others had not given, but for what she had been forced to take for herself. They were grateful tears. The struggle was over. Thanks to a mouthful of pain relievers, the cramping was now cooking at a low simmer.

She remembered the cold brown-tinged water she used to have to bathe in. The gas heater in the daylight basement would conk out all the time and the pipes were rusty.

Back then, baby Montana was hungry. The monthly ration of food stamps was often sold off for fifty cents on the dollar to pay the light bill. A bill collector would call six times a day about a 1985 Honda that was sitting on bricks in the backyard. Even if she had the means, she flat out refused to pay the note when she had to take two buses and a train to school. The phone was disconnected anyway and, if they wanted it, they could come and drag it off with a tow truck.

The landlord promised to send a serviceman to see after the water heater and the pipes if she stuck to the arrangements to pay the rent and late fees. When the plumber arrived, he took one look at then three-year-old Montana and eyed an opportunity. He could fix the unit, he explained, but it needed a new part. If she'd give him a little something extra for his trouble, he might be inclined to order it and return the next day. If she was especially generous, he could get new pipes too and flush the lines. Thandy didn't have any extra money, she explained. Everything she had was promised to the landlord. He unzipped his trousers and his pants fell down to his knees. Thandy grabbed a butcher's knife and chased him out. He tripped on the pavement as he tried to get back to his truck.

When he was gone, she went next door to Phillipa's house and called the landlord again. He was unmoved. Phillipa told Thandy to report him to the county housing authority. She did, but the old man found a way to pay her back for causing him trouble. He filed an eviction notice and shut off the power. That day, Phillipa, the one friend she was willing to tell, helped her move into an extended stay hotel. Even then, she was too proud to take the spare room in Phillipa's basement. The hotel was just temporary, she promised herself.

Later that night, alone in the hotel, she broke down. She cried like it was her first and last time to do so. She promised herself it would be over soon, like she knew it for certain. She told herself that she was destined for greatness. But Thandy knew the truth was that while she was waiting on God, He was waiting on her. He was waiting for her to make a decision to either get on with the life that was meant for her or be choked to death by the one she was living. "*Pick up your mat and walk,*" she heard Him say. She heard it as clear as the sunrise.

Her father-in-law refused her pleas for help and even went as far as to blame her for his son's imprisonment. Her own mother didn't return her calls. Before he died, her father had answered once and promptly hung up. She'd sent dozens of letters over the years and none had been answered. She was too proud to call her sister Yvonne, who was sadly not much different from saintly Yvetta.

Thandy still had nightmares of Monty's arrest on their living room floor and Montana's screams. She still had pangs of guilt about what she had to do to save their daughter.

Montana had been sent to foster care while Thandy sat in jail. She called Big Boy's lawyer. Getting Montana back would mean cutting a deal against her own husband, finding a job and a decent place to live, the attorney explained. Under the circumstances, he couldn't represent them both. His advice, he said, was friend to friend. He gave her a number for one of his colleagues.

On the advice of counsel, she testified for two days, choking back tears as her husband sat at the defense table.

Forgive me, she mouthed.

It's alright, baby, he said back.

She lost everything. She packed all she could into the backseat of the Honda she bought at a "buy here, pay here" lot and drove off to nowhere. Several months later, after the eviction, after a four-week stay in a hotel, she found a new apartment and went back to school, reenrolling at Georgia State, completing another two semesters funded by federal Pell grants and guaranteed student loans.

On a leap of faith and at the urging of her academic advisor, Sloane Faulkner, she filed a transfer application at Emory University. The form never asked if she had ever been charged with a felony. Thandy didn't feel compelled to tell them. She spent weeks writing and rewriting the required personal essay. "*I am a welfare mother,*" it started. "*Those words alone evoke a whole host of vicious stereotypes. But more than that, I am a dedicated mother and a scholar. My name is Thandywaye Mbeki Malone.*"

A few months later, she clutched the acceptance letter; excited and scared, she ran straight to Sloane with the news. She couldn't afford the books and fees, let alone the twenty thousand in tuition. Georgia State had been free thanks to the government aid, which she wouldn't have qualified for if she had been convicted. Thandy read and reread the phrase "need blind." Sloane explained that since she had been accepted, the university would marshal the resources to pay for her tuition. Scholarships, grants, and work-study programs would all be cobbled together to meet the bill.

She enrolled in classes that fall and landed a job at the A&P grocery store a few blocks off campus, earning a little more than minimum wage. Health insurance would have cost half her small paycheck, so she checked a box declining coverage. Montana was back at home where she belonged. Nothing else mattered.

No insurance meant Montana would have to get her immunizations at the public clinic. But she was feeling liberated then. She was just happy to have her baby home. It was an honest day's work for an honest day's pay, just as Granddaddy Cump had advised. She moved into University Apartments off Clairmont Road, where the rent was more manageable and included in her school fees. Although no one noticed it at the time, Thandy was far and beyond smarter than her high school peers. The rudiments of basic algebra and English composition presented no significant challenge. Despite her natural brilliance, she'd been written off early as she gazed out the window of the classroom, unwilling to participate in the charade of acting as if she was learning something.

She regretted that now. The only thing that stood between her and the stability she craved for her daughter was a collection of advanced math classes and seminars in international business. Thandy had no one to please but herself. She completed undergraduate studies with a major in finance the following year, then applied to law school. She didn't really have an interest in practicing law, but her life with Monty had taught her one thing: if money is involved there had better be a clean, enforceable paper trail.

Fellowship offers came from across the country. She wouldn't leave Emory, not even if Harvard called. She took a job as a staff accountant at a small but prestigious firm run by a former Atlanta mayor while attending Emory Law and dually enrolled in the Business School. Despite the demands of her new job, she graduated third in her class.

Over the next four years, she rose quickly through the

ranks. When she was later offered a new position at a larger firm, the former mayor wished her well and called from time to time to check in. Thandy made her mark fast and was named chief customer officer at McDonough, Press, and Sweet Asset Management.

It was then that she met Jack.

He was tall, generously handsome, and completely caught up with her. She had been hesitant at first. After all, he was very much married. It wasn't long before Jack gained her trust, won her heart. Charismatic and something just short of brilliant, for a while, Jack simply lost himself in Thandy and she let him. She marveled at the things he knew, the places he had been. Night after night, she laid her head in his lap as he took her on a tour of the world she had not yet seen. He was full of promises then. She learned to deal with his marriage and never once pressed for a divorce. *A man does what he wants to do every day*, she told herself.

In the beginning, Jack was overly supportive and for a time she was satisfied with the time he carved out for her. He purchased and moved her into a high-rise condominium and bought her a new car, payment for some indiscretion she had no clue he'd committed.

Resting high above Peachtree Road, Park Place Towers remains one of the city's most prestigious addresses. Home to Sir Elton John, Janet Jackson, and Coretta Scott King, Thandy at first felt uneasy with Jack's generosity. The three-bedroom, two-story unit boasted crisp white walls, cherry stained hardwoods, and granite counter tops. The wraparound balcony looked out onto the Atlanta skyline. As her career progressed, she applied for a mortgage and attempted to repay Jack for his kindness. He declined the money and told her it was a birthday gift.

"But my birthday isn't for another three months."

"Every day is your birthday when you're with me," he declared.

Thandy longed for the days when he would cancel his appointments and spend the day with her walking the trails of Piedmont Park or taking a drive all the way to Savannah to stuff their mouths with crabmeat and low boiled shrimp. She wanted to cook for him, to watch him eat. She missed his laugh, the way he gently kneaded the knots out of her neck. Jack had been particular about what he wanted. So she gave up eating red meat and let her hair grow even longer to please him. There was no room for imperfection, no room for exceptions. She had let him see nothing less than the best of her.

When her father died in the summer of 2001, Jack drove her to North Carolina to attend the funeral services. As then twelve-year-old Montana slept in the backseat, they quietly talked about a future, maybe more children. They held hands for nearly the entire drive. Thandy allowed herself to stop talking and fell asleep. She felt safe with him. She hadn't felt so safe in a very long time, not since Monty went away. But that was then. Thandy now believed that the talk of marriage and children had been a ploy meant to keep her in close quarters. The house and car were expensive bribes, she reasoned. As long as hope was alive, he could keep stringing her along.

Hyde Park is a long way from Decatur, Georgia, Thandy realized, as the warm water ran over her. Montana was now sleeping comfortably in a bedroom at the far end of the hall with an early admission acceptance letter from Yale taped to her bathroom mirror. The house she lived in now was not a gift, but something she had earned for herself. She was careful not to bring anything with her that Jack had purchased. The vestiges of their life together had been donated to the Atlanta Furniture Bank in his name. In time, she hoped, Jack would become a distant memory, as inconsequential as a late-night infomercial. She didn't even have a picture of them together. Jack would never allow one to be taken.

Thandy knew Monty would be proud of them both. He was still locked up downstate in Marion, not more than four hours away. She never visited him. Monty didn't want her there. He didn't want his daughter to know him that way. Although she never avoided the conversation, she and Montana simply hadn't talked about him much over the years. But she wanted Montana to know her father and to know how good he had been to them.

She lathered and rinsed her hair, letting the warm suds run down her body. She stayed there for a while, thankful for the clean hot water, glad to be alive, glad for the little things. She heard music coming from down the hallway. The bathroom walls pulsed. Montana was still awake, blasting the new Kanye West CD from her stereo.

"Now I ain't sayin' she a gold digger."

A parental alarm went off in Thandy's head. While she herself was young enough to have been raised on hip-hop, there were still some things she could not stomach. She hated the word nigger.

"Turn that crap off! Montana!"

The music went down.

"What did you say?"

"I said, turn that stereo off!" she said, sticking her head through the shower curtain.

"But, Mom!"

"But, Mom nothing! I said turn it off!"

Two seconds later, the music changed.

"God show me the way because the Devil trying to break me down."

Thandy caught herself bobbing her head despite herself. The long, wet strands of dark hair flapped against her back. She danced in the warm, clean water.

Thandy shook her head and stepped onto the bathroom floor. It was always "nigger this" and "nigger that." Cump, a child of the Jim Crow-era South, never allowed anyone to utter it in his presence. No one would be brought low by that word. But now she had a top floor view. She could hardly believe what she had accomplished. If someone had told her even fifteen years ago that she would become the president of a world-renowned wealth management practice, she would have called them a liar. But her day had come and she loved the very taste of it.

As she got out of the shower, a sharp, stabbing pain caught her between her legs and ripped up and through her abdomen like a twisting knife. She fumbled through the shower curtain and got out of the water. She broke down on her hands and knees, burying her face in the tile floor, and howled. She crawled across the floor. Blood poured from between her legs. She pulled a towel from the rack and moaned.

"Jesus walks . . ."

Muddy blood rolled down her legs and onto the floor, staining the grout and tiles. She alternatively grunted and moaned as the pains grew more intense. "Somebody help me," she muttered.

Wet and naked, Thandy pulled herself together and tried to clean up the blood with the bath towel. Her abdomen was throbbing. She hadn't noticed the trickles of blood in the shower stall. She got on her feet and felt her way through the dark bedroom and into the hallway.

"Montana!" she called. "Monty, baby, come quick!"

The music was still blaring. *"Jesus walks with me . . ."*

"Monty!" she shrieked. "Uhn!" Thandy doubled over and collapsed.

Montana moved quickly. She dressed her mother in a pair of sweatpants and a T-shirt, snatched the keys from the hook in the kitchen, and drove her mother to the emergency room. The University of Chicago Medical Center was just a few blocks away. It was so close that the anesthesiologist, who lived next door, often biked to work. Montana blew through four stop signs and hit a hard right into the emergency entrance. Two orderlies appeared with a wheelchair and helped Thandy from the car.

"I'm coming with you."

"Stay here," her mother demanded.

Montana paced the waiting room for hours, stopping only to answer a nurse's questions.

"She's thirty-four," Montana said. "No allergies. No history of heart trouble."

"Any history of diabetes? Anemia?"

She apologized, vigorously shook her head, and said she didn't know much about her mother's past.

Finding out that her mother had been pregnant wasn't such bad news. It was just an evil reminder that nothing about this life had been good for too long. Montana went home long enough to retrieve her mother's nightclothes. At home, she scrubbed the blood from the carpet in the hallway, mopped the tile floor, then returned to sleep the night at her mother's bedside. Montana had a thousand questions whirling around in her head. She didn't even know her mother had a boyfriend. She also wanted to know something, anything about her own father. She didn't even know his name.

Chapter 14

The phone woke her, but she didn't pick it up. Jack was still sleeping. She reached over and took the phone off the hook. She snuggled in close and wrapped her body around his, her generous breasts pushed against his back.

He hadn't planned to stay the night. But then again, Jack hadn't planned to get involved with a cocktail waitress who had an overly sensitive nose for old money. But the sex was good and he was too tired to go home. It was still dark when he got up. Her little black dress was on the floor, right where he'd tossed it. She was still naked, Jack was sure of that.

Angel Delafuenta was a mildly pretty but well-stacked girl, with near waist-length hair and grass green eyes. Streetwise, she was raised in the dirt and weeds of East Camden, New Jersey. Her father, James Bedford, was a retired Marine staff sergeant and her mother was a pretty Mexican girl he met on a three-day junket to Tijuana. After twelve turbulent years of marriage, he abruptly left his family of five girls and one boy after a wild night with a Puerto Rican stripper who had big breasts and a pencil-thin waistline. Angel helped her mother rear her younger siblings in a two-bedroom, one-bath shotgun house. Risa Delafuenta and her daughters cleaned houses and put away enough money to send all of the Bedford children to college.

Angel managed to get an associate's degree in accounting, between scrubbing toilets and dropping her father's last name. Bedford wasn't sexy enough. She never forgave James Bedford for leaving and she never saw him again. When he was murdered during a barroom brawl somewhere near Wichita, Kansas, the Social Security Administration began sending widow's and survivors' benefits. The Veteran's Administration forwarded his retirement payments and the proceeds from his military life insurance policy. Risa gave Angel the first two allotment checks and pressed her to get out of East Camden.

Angel moved to Atlanta in 1999 in search of a new job and a new life. Early on, she slipped into easy drugs and something just short of casual sex. Money was no problem. There was always one man or another willing to pay the rent and she efficiently fucked her way toward financial stability. When that dried up, she took a job waiting tables at Café 420, a makeshift jazz club on the east side of town that welcomed twenty-something wannabes. She served cheap champagne and Long Island Iced Teas dressed in a tuxedo shirt, black shorts, fishnets, and stilettos in the velvet-roped VIP section. The tips, like the drinks, were always watered down.

Her luck got better when a physician's group leased out the nightclub on Sunday nights for a once a month social. Jack Gabrielle, the leader of the pack, had been her favorite customer. He always sat in a far corner, above the crowd, where he could watch the beautiful women. His shoes and watch shone with old money. To Angel, it was the best kind. He was obviously out of his element.

The small brick bungalow she lived in was cramped and smelled like cherry incense and candle wax. The furnishings were inexpensive, but neatly kept. Everything had a place.

The running shower woke her up. Angel joined him. Her smile was bright and expectant.

"Listen, let's get one thing straight," he said as he dried off with a fresh towel he found in her linen closet. "We've got to let things cool off."

"You don't have to do this alone," she purred, wrapping her arms around his still wet body.

"This won't help," he said easing away. "Look, in another month or so, it will all be over."

"We'll have to celebrate," she cooed.

"Whatever."

"What does that mean?" Angel asked, trying not to be offended.

"That means when this is over we can celebrate."

She needed to hear him say it. *After the divorce, it's all yours. Nothing but the best for you, my love.*

Rather than a steamy I-won't-be-gone-long send-off, he pecked her on the cheek and left.

By 6:15 a.m., Jack was standing in line at a crowded Starbucks a few blocks from his house.

"Good morning, Dr. G!" the girl at the counter sang, handing him a cup of relief. "How's Mrs. G?"

"Just groovy," he answered as he gripped the hot cup. "She's just groovy. Visiting family."

For the first time, he bothered to look at the side of his cup and read the Jill Scott quote: "*Embrace this right now life . . . Capture these times because it will soon be very different.*"

His eyes were red, his thoughts blurry. But one thing was clear. At some point during the night with Angel, and again as he read the singer's words, he'd made the decision to find Thandy. He'd take her to a fancy restaurant, get on his knees, and apologize. He'd tell her about Etienne filing for divorce. He assured himself that he could turn everything around. He'd get to know Montana, maybe see her off to college. He'd give Thandy everything he'd promised. Jack had never known someone so beautiful, someone who wanted him for him, not for what he had. He could think of no one else who would hand him back a million-dollar house and a Mercedes-Benz.

Jack drained his coffee as he scanned the morning *Atlanta Journal-Constitution* and tossed the empty cup into the trash receptacle. He went home and quickly changed clothes.

Wearing well-worn, starched khaki pants, a pullover polo shirt, and a baseball cap, Jack walked into his lawyer's office. Framed degrees from Harvard lined the walls. The credenza was covered with family pictures in pewter frames. Skip Parham, sitting behind his majestic carved-wood desk, had been waiting for this day. The retainer had been paid over a decade ago.

He looked down at his notes, sighed, and said, "She won't sign."

"What do you mean 'she won't sign'?" Jack said incredulously.

"She won't sign the offer. Your wife wants more money."

Jack sat up ramrod in his chair and asked, "How much?"

"Triple."

Jack swallowed. "Fifteen million! For what?"

"She's not stupid," Parham said. "Finlayson says if we don't take the counteroffer, he will amend the filing."

"With what?"

"Adultery, for starters."

"She can't be serious." Jack's stomach was doing somersaults off the high beam.

"Under the circumstances, I think we should consider it. Adultery means fifty percent of everything in addition to spousal and child support payments."

"Half? Half of *my* money?"

"Finlayson seems to think you've got money squired away in the Islands. He mentioned a condominium he believes you purchased for a mistress."

"Damn." Jack was sweating.

He leaned back in his chair. His shoulders slumped. Etienne knew about Barbados and she knew Thandy's phone number. What else she knew was anybody's guess. Surely, she didn't know *where* to find his money. That's what numbered accounts are for.

Jack's eyes began to dart around the room. He nervously bit his thumbnail off and asked, "Where are my boys?"

"My guess is that she's hiding them. We checked out her mother's townhouse. No sign of them. I don't think they made the flight to Washington. Finlayson filed for temporary custody. The judge is inclined to agree under the circumstances."

Bitch. She wants my money and my boys, Jack said to himself. He didn't need to say it out loud. Parham heard it.

"What circumstances?" Jack asked.

"You work a hundred hours a week and your travel schedule would kill a man half your age. Your wife contends you spend less than ten hours a month with your sons. But the court won't look favorably on her actions. Judges don't like it when parents hide children and she's doing a mighty fine job of it."

"Damn."

"Look, I'll get our investigator to step up the search for the boys. No doubt they're still in the city. I'll need the names and addresses of any family in the area, girlfriends, etc. This afternoon, I'll file a countersuit."

Jack leaned out of his chair and took a pen from Parham's desk. "With what?" he asked, scribbling down the most suspect among her friends.

Etienne's sorority sister Abigail Stewart topped the list. He never liked the bitch anyway. Jack had a good mind to drive down to her house, but getting arrested wasn't on his list of things to do that day.

"We can charge abandonment. You say she drinks like a fish, so we'll throw in drug addiction and mental abuse. We'll charge her with hiding the boys and alienation of affection."

"What's that?"

"You said there's been no sex for almost two years. We'll blame it on her. In the meantime, I'll get a restraining order barring her from the house."

Atta boy!

"This could go long. You sure you don't want to just pay her?"

"Let me think about it. I'm trying not to write a check for fifteen large. I'll call you before the day is over."

Parham paused. "Who's the girl?"

"What girl?"

"The one you bought the condo for."

The pang of regret came again. "Her name is Thandy. Thandywaye Malone."

"Where is she now?"

"I guess she just wised up and left me."

"Don't tell me this is all about a woman."

"A man is only as faithful as his options."

"Or at least the options he thinks he has."

By 10:00 a.m., he had seen a bevy of patients and waved off a pretty pharmaceutical rep hawking samples of a new wonder drug. She was dressed in a tight blouse and a pair of slacks he was certain she painted on. He shooed her out of his office and promised to phone in an order. He sat at his desk long enough to log online and order a dozen long-stemmed red roses. He searched the Campbell-Perkins Web site and found the address for the home office in Chicago. A photo of Thandy appeared on the home page. He punched the link and a flattering bio appeared. "Thandywaye Malone and her daughter Montana reside in Hyde Park," the last and most troublesome line read. At least he knew where to find her.

He went to flowers.com and plugged in the newly acquired office address and his credit card number. He took the next-day delivery option. He might have ferried them there himself if he didn't have four days of surgeries lined up. Sandy tapped on his office door to remind him there were more patients. By noon, Angel had called his cell phone three times and left four messages with his office. He pressed ignore, balled up and threw the message slips in the wastebasket, and went to lunch.

Chapter 15

The cafeteria at Northside Hospital was brimming with medical staff and patient families looking for a midday reprieve. The room was as noisy as a Wednesday night happy hour. Jack took his tray and sat next to Seth Martin, a young associate from his practice. He was lucky to land a talent like Dr. Martin, he thought.

The young physician, ten years his junior, graduated at the top of his class from Morehouse College and went on to do the same at Johns Hopkins School of Medicine. His credentials were impeccable, his passion and zeal for medicine unmatched. Affectionately known as Doogie, Martin graduated from Marshall High School on Chicago's South Side at fifteen, college at eighteen, and then went on to medical school, where he simultaneously earned a Ph.D. in biophysics. He later completed his surgical residency at Sloan-Kettering in New York under the watchful eye of Dr. Howard Kellman, himself the father of two physician sons. A compulsive academic by nature, Doogie taught accelerated biophysics to premed students at Morehouse several mornings a week, ran a chemistry tutorial on Wednesday evenings, and was on staff at the National Center for Primary Care at Morehouse School of Medicine. He had been handpicked by former Surgeon General David Satcher, the founding director of the Center and interim president of the medical school. Doogie was president-elect and soon-to-be chairman of the Atlanta Medical Association, a post proudly and previously held by The Great Jack Gabrielle. At thirty-seven, Doogie had written dozens of articles on the disparities of health care for minorities and was appointed by the president to chair a White House commission dedicated to the issue. Two years ago, the Atlanta Medical Association named him "Young Physician of the Year." More than a physician, Doogie was committed to something far greater. If he had his way, he would increase the quality of and access to health care for every person of color in the country.

Jack believed he could do it from the moment he laid eyes on him.

Their conversation meandered around minutia as they ate cold cut sandwiches and gulped down Styrofoam cups of lemonade.

"I hear you're getting a divorce," Doogie finally said.

"Yeah," Jack paused. "Long time coming."

"These things can get nasty. Are you ready for that?"

"No one is ever truly ready."

"Do you regret it?"

"Regret what?"

"Getting married."

"No. Not really," Jack shrugged.

"What's it like?"

"Doogie my man, marriage is like having a very wonderful dessert, before a very long, tortured dinner."

"Can't be that bad, can it?" Doogie asked with hope.

"They all look good on paper. She's holding out for more money," Jack threw out.

"Wouldn't you?"

"Maybe," Jack shrugged.

"I'm sorry to get in your business."

"Shit happens. What about you? Aren't you engaged?"

"Yeah, I am. I just hope that I picked the right one. I burned

through a lot of women before I met her. My mother is still trying to hook me up with some woman from her church," he
laughed.

"What does your fiancée do for a living?" Jack asked.

"She's a writer."

"Out of work, huh?"

They laughed.

"Stephanie says I work too much."

"She might have a point. Never believe you did the picking,
Doogie. They always pick us."

"True that. She's fantastic. You'll have to meet her."

Jack finished his sandwich, dabbed the crumbs from his lips,
said good-bye, and headed for the elevator. He took the pedestrian bridge back to his office. The heavy soles slapped the marble tiling liked a rapping drum, his heart thumping. Sandy had
the afternoon fully booked and put him right to work. He slid
into his lab coat.

"Let's get to it," he said.

A young woman strolled into the office like she owned the place.

"Do you have an appointment?" Sandy asked, peering over
her wire-rimmed glasses.

"I'm a friend," Angel said dryly.

Sandy frowned. "He's in with patients right now. Can I take
your name and give him a message?"

"Just tell him I'm here."

"He's in with a patient," Sandy pointed out again. "You'll have
to make an appointment."

The young woman would be cute, if she had any class, Sandy
thought. As Angel removed her sunglasses, Sandy was struck by
her deep green eyes. They were smart, mischievous eyes. Yet
Sandy knew her type by her cheap "come-fuck-me" pumps. Why
Dr. Gabrielle would waste his time, Sandy didn't know. But this
was her turf and the nurse wasted no time letting the young
woman know it.

"What's your name, ma'am?"

"Ms. Delafuenta. D-E-L . . ."

"I know how to spell it," Sandy spit out.

Bitch, Angel wanted to say. *You better know how to spell it.*

Between patients, Sandy slipped Jack the note.

"Your *friend* is a pushy little something," she warned. "She called at least four times today and then came in."

"Where is she now?" Jack asked with little patience.

"In the waiting room."

Jack went immediately to the front office, threw open the door and summoned Angel back to his office. He slammed the door behind her.

"Did you not hear one word of what I told you this morning? You can't be here. Didn't you get that? I told you we had to cool this thing off." His fury was barely contained.

Angel crossed her shapely bronze legs and sat coolly as he fired away. She remained cucumber cool as he came unglued. She said finally, "Jack, I'm pregnant."

"You are undoubtedly the most . . ." he stopped midsentence. "With what?"

"A baby."

"Whose baby?"

"Jack, don't be funny. With *our* baby."

"*We* are not having a baby."

"What do you want me to do?"

"Get rid of it. I'll call a colleague and arrange for it this afternoon."

"It? You can't be serious." Her green doe eyes began to tear.

"I could not be more serious."

His fingers were tingling with rage.

"If you don't mind, I need some time to think," he growled.

"Sure Jack. Anything you want," she said sweetly.

"And while I'm doing that, I want you to call a friend of mine," he said scribbling a colleague's name and number on a pad. "His name is Bill Whitehead. He's a gynecologist. He'll give you a blood test."

"For what?"

"To confirm you're actually pregnant."

Angel thought quickly. "I don't mind taking a test. That's not what's important. I just need to know you want us—me and the baby."

"Angel, tell me you love me with a straight face. Tell me it's not the fancy cars, the trips, and all the money that you love. Tell me you don't love the idea of a big house. Tell me you wouldn't do just about anything to stop waiting tables."

He snapped off his watch and threw it into her lap.

"Take it. It's worth at least thirty grand."

"My job pays my bills," she said, tilting her head up. "I don't need anything from you. Jack, you know that I love you."

"I knew we would get around to that. Tell me you'd love me if I was broke," he demanded.

Angel tossed her generous hair back and said innocently, "I didn't want to make things complicated."

"Too late for that," he sniped.

She took the slip of paper, placed the watch on his desk, and left.

Jack instructed Sandy to cancel the afternoon's patients and send those that were already there to Doogie and the other associates. Long after Angel had gone, Jack sat in his office behind locked doors for hours waiting for the answer. He didn't like Angel's idea of a happy family. Eight months ago, she was just another girl with a tasty set of lips who knew how to keep them closed. She was a quick and easy detour whenever Thandy was out of town or busy working. For a while, she was so wrapped up visiting colleges with Montana and volunteering for the campaign that she was rarely home.

There had been others, including Lucy the Lunatic, a manic-depressive who showed up unannounced on his doorstep with her suitcases. He kept her supplied with lithium. When she was lucid, Lucy would bake him lasagna and cook homemade meatballs. When she wasn't, she'd call his cell phone a hundred times a day and threaten suicide if he didn't come over right away. When he didn't return her calls, he would invariably find that she'd keyed his Porsche. Etienne was suspicious, but Jack blamed the incidents on schoolkid pranks. Lucy flattened eight tires and broke out the windows of his BMW before it was all said and done.

Then there was Sugar. Just the thought of her made his head spin. She didn't need any other name—just Sugar. They made love efficiently so she could get home in time to cook dinner for her husband, whom Jack knew in passing. Jack had been her escape; he was her one indulgence. Their frequent rendezvous at a local no-tell-motel usually lasted under thirty minutes. In and out with no strings. Sugar didn't know and didn't care what Jack did for a living until she saw him interviewed on CNN one afternoon. Even then, she didn't mention it. A couple of years back, she joined a new church and abruptly stopped calling. Where was Sugar when he could use a cup?

If you lined them all up in a row, you could scarcely tell one from the other. They could pass for first cousins, if not sisters. All had long raven hair, light-colored eyes, and skin like butter. Etienne would have stood out like a sore thumb. Far from light-bright-almost-white, Etienne's toasted pecan complexion and deep coal black eyes were a sharp contradiction to Jack's paramours. But at the time, the marriage looked good on paper. Once a sure-footed society diva, his wife was the scion of an important family and needed little training in Wife 101. *Why do I always pick the crazy ones?*

Another hour went by before his private line rang.

"It's positive."

Jack accepted the news without question.

"Thanks, Whitey. I owe you one."

"Who is she?"

"Just a friend in need."

Chapter 16

L ate on Election Day night, a handful of county offices in the southeast corner of Georgia were still counting votes, but the race for governor was decidedly a landslide. The loser, as is customary, made the obligatory phone call to pledge his support. The concession lasted less than two minutes.

The crowd was cheering and the champagne was flowing when Sloane Faulkner took the stage. It was closing in on 2:00 a.m. when the final vote came in. He'd waited in a hotel suite high above the ballroom, surrounded by the campaign team and family. They waited until there was little or no doubt left. He was the people's man; the one they could call on when the garbage man wouldn't pick up bad furniture; when City Hall didn't pick up the phone; when the lady at the voting booth tried to deny their God-given right to cast a vote. Faulkner was their man.

In another life, he had been an unassuming high school physics teacher and taught evening classes at Georgia State. A nasty zoning fight lured him down to City Hall. A big-box retailer threatened to put a store in the neighborhood. They didn't expect Sloane and Marla Faulkner. Together, they rallied their neighbors and told the corporate stiffs to go to hell. Savoring the victory, he didn't leave City Hall for nearly twelve years.

The hotly contested race for governor would have been a run-of-the-mill scrap, but Faulkner wouldn't take a dive. He went on campaigning like he could win the thing. The incumbent had a fat war chest and endorsements from anybody who meant anything. Two weeks before Election Day, his wily opponent produced a stack of ill-gotten tax records and proudly announced that Sloane Faulkner was a fraud. According to the IRS, Faulkner owed more than $200,000 in back taxes. Never mind that he'd lost four times that on a bad land deal. How could he manage the state's business when he couldn't see after his own?

Faulkner was better at math than the IRS. Three days later, he held up a letter showing a reversal. The Federal agency actually owed *him* $40,000. The campaign committee, armed with hundreds of volunteers, redoubled their efforts. The people had the final say.

"The only poll that counts is the one they take on Election Day," Faulkner told the baptized masses.

He eased up to the podium, with his dutiful wife and grown children at his side, and claimed the victory. It had been a long time coming. The first race for Atlanta city council had been a decided cakewalk. He doubled down and ran for council president in the next cycle. There was no stopping Faulkner. The road had been well paved. Four years ago, Faulkner made history when he soundly defeated a sitting lieutenant governor, a mostly ceremonious post that included more than his share of ribbon cuttings at senior citizen's centers, and fried chicken dinners in church basements. His intentions were as clear as tea leaves even then. Faulkner was on a mission. He would become the first black governor south of the Mason-Dixon Line. He alone would stop the Republican tide rolling across the South.

"To the people of Georgia, I say thank you!" Faulkner began.

The crowd roared as they waved signs emblazoned with his name. The governor-elect cleared his throat. He raised his hands over the audience and they at once grew silent.

"You went to the polls this morning and told the world that you won't be nailed down. That you won't give up or give in. You said you were tired of dirty politics and secret backdoor deals. You told us that you're ready to fight for a better Georgia!"

The crowd went wild. When the noise subsided, he continued on. "And I'll tell you one more thing," he boomed.

"Make it plain!" a woman yelled from the back.

"Yes, ma'am!" he returned. "This is *our* Georgia. Black, white, brown, and otherwise. Rich, poor, and somewhere in between. Man, woman, and child. Republican and Democrat, this is our Georgia!"

"Say it, son!" another woman shouted.

"I want you to know that I heard you this morning. The entire country heard you. Hell, the entire world heard you!"

He paused and said, "They heard you say, this is your Georgia!"

The crowd began to chant. "Faulkner! Faulkner!"

"I mean to tell you that you did a good thing this morning. You went to the polls and made your voice heard."

He lowered his voice.

"That, my friends, is a powerful thing. Fifty-nine years ago, my mother told me that there was a brighter day ahead. Even as she scrubbed floors for four dollars a day, she pressed me to do better. When my daddy got laid off from the carpet mill in Dalton, she told us to move on. She told me that I need only look to Tallulah Falls, that I need only see the glory of Stone Mountain. That I need only know that power of the great Chattahoochee River. That I need only look to the valleys of Albany, the streets of Atlanta, the piedmonts of Habersham, the shores of Savannah, to hear the sweet music of our native son Ray Charles. *'Georgia! Georgia!'*" he sang. "I need only look there to see the promise of a better day!"

The crowd lit up. *"It's just an old sweet song. Georgia on my mind,"* they sang in unison.

"When I announced my candidacy for governor of this great state, wiser minds called me a fool! They said I was a crazy man. A deranged physics teacher."

"Say it ain't so!"

"Yes, sir," he said to the crowd. "They said I didn't have enough money. They said I didn't have the experience. That I didn't have the support. I ain't ashamed to tell you they said no black man was worthy of this esteemed office. That Georgia hadn't come far enough."

"No, they didn't!"

"But, Lord, Lord, Lord. I tell you the truth. You told them they were wrong! As surely as the sun rises over Brunswick and sets over Villa Rica."

"Yeah!"

"You told them that you knew better!"

"Yeah!"

"You told them that we were ready for better schools! A better economy! Better jobs! Meaningful jobs at meaningful wages! Something you can raise your children on! Better housing! A government that serves the people!"

"Yeah!"

"They said, look here, Faulkner. Those are good ideas, but ain't no way you can win. The big boys won't give you their money. Rural Georgia will turn their back on you. Atlanta won't turn out. They'll cut you off at the pass. They won't let you by. But surely, so surely as the Chattahoochee rolls downstream, I stand before you tonight as your next governor!"

The audience erupted. Marla Faulkner beamed.

"It is with honor and gratitude that I stand before you tonight and say thank you. Thank you to Mrs. Idela Young from White County who mailed a five-dollar bill to the campaign. Thank you to Mr. Agner Pope from Columbia County who called me at two o'clock in the morning to say, 'keep your head up and keep going.' Thank you to Mrs. Lila Brown and her bridge club in Winder for going door-to-door, urging their neighbors to give me their support. You welcomed me at the Unadilla Kiwanis Club and the Rotary Club in Macon. I had breakfast with you at a diner in Helen. You opened your homes and your hearts. I tell you that it meant all the difference. And darling," he said, pulling Marla in close. "You make the difference every day."

The crowd roared.

Sloane and Marla Faulkner had been married over twenty-five years. Both had been schoolteachers. Together, they raised three daughters: 24-year-old Misha was in law school at the University of Georgia, and the younger twins, Mavis and Marla, were co-eds at Georgia Tech studying software engineering. All were campaign volunteers. They stood beside their father, convinced he was the smartest man they ever knew. Various campaign staffers lined up behind them. Others scurried in and out of the hotel ballroom directing media traffic and rechecking the numbers. All four local broadcast affiliates were carrying the event live from the ballroom.

Thandy was lying in bed, watching proudly as others took the podium. Her best friend and former college professor was making history. She leapt up from the mattress and pumped her fists in the air. He'd won!

Thandy had hosted a fundraiser at her firm and opened her home to friends. Jack came, too. One of the early naysayers, he had been slow to believe, although he wrote a check for the maximum contribution only because Sloane was his friend, too.

They spent the evening pretending they were casual friends. Phillipa would have riddled his body with darts, but Thandy forbade it. Her guests sipped wine and nibbled at small plates of hors d'oeuvres as they crowded into her living room. Sloane had been simply magical, if not enchanting that evening. Each of the over ninety guests stroked a check for the maximum contribution. At her direction the National Association of Securities Professionals' political action committee made a handsome donation of twenty thousand dollars which Thandy delivered personally. All told, her efforts brought in over two hundred thousand. Just after four o'clock in the morning, her phone rang.

"Girl, we did it!" Sloane said.

"No, my friend, you did it," she yawned and stretched her arms. "I haven't slept in two days."

Thandy pinned the phone between her cheek and shoulder. "I know it was worth it."

"Every minute. How are you? How is Chicago?"

"Chicago is good. I'm just waiting for the first snow," she yawned again, pouring her vowels out like a waterfall in slow motion. "I miss Atlanta."

"Every good-bye ain't gone."

"That means some are and maybe that's for the better."

"How is Montana? Is she ready for Yale?"

"The real question is can Yale get ready for her?" She could sense his smile through the phone.

"How are you? Really?"

"I'm good," she said wiping the crust out of her eyes. "I promise."

"It's late. I know I woke you up, but I just wanted to hear your voice."

"It's good to hear yours."

"Dating?"

"Not really. Just fumbling around I guess. Chicago does have its charms."

"You know, Thandy, fumbling around until the right thing comes along can be good. Fumbling is good. Sit still long enough and the right man will find you. You ain't hard to miss."

"The guy next door brought a welcome basket by the other day."

"I'm sure he did," Sloane said with a chuckle. "Did you invite him in?"

"Of course not," Thandy scrunched her brows. Sloane knew better.

"He's probably still waiting outside," Sloane laughed again.

"I hear what you're saying but I'm not ready. I don't know that I have anything to give anybody."

"Any man in his right mind would be glad to be yours. Promise me you'll find the time to get out there and fumble some."

"That's easier said than done."

"I know. Phillipa tells me that you had a medical emergency of some sort."

"It was nothing really. I spent the night in the hospital. Just tired, I guess. Bad substitute for a vacation."

"Why didn't you call me?" Worry laced his voice.

"Nothing you could do from Atlanta. You had a campaign to win."

"With no small thanks to you. Anything I can do?"

"I'm okay. Really I am."

"What happened?"

Thandy paused for a moment and said, "Seems I was pregnant."

"God, no!"

"I had a miscarriage."

"Are you all right, baby-girl?"

"It was for the best. And you're right. I just need to move on. The good Lord has a way of taking care of these things. Every moment is as it should be."

"I'm sorry."

She eased down into the blankets and closed her eyes.

"Don't be. Like I said, every moment is as it should be and I believe that. After I get through this, I will fumble around a little more. I promise."

"You know I knew you were something special the day you walked into my classroom. I knew you were going to do big things."

"I remember. Montana had chicken pox."

"And you brought her to class with you."

"No other choice. If we were going to get up and get on, I couldn't stay away from class. I guess she went to Emory, too."

He laughed. "They ought to give her an honorary degree."

"She'll have to get her own."

"She will. Trust me on that. Did you hear my speech tonight?"

"You know I did. CNN carried it live. They even mentioned it on the local station up here. I wanted to be there with you."

"You were. You tend to leave a mark. Jack came by headquarters last night. He was asking after you. He wanted to know if you were doing okay. I told him you were."

"Like you said, it will be better if I just move on."

"You know that he loves you."

"I don't believe that."

"You don't have to. It just is."

"He never said it."

Sloane sighed. "I know it had to be hard on you to walk away. But I know you did what you thought was right."

"He was never good about keeping his promises."

"You know he wanted to give you the world, but he just didn't know how."

"No, Sloane. He wouldn't."

"And you just let that be his mistake."

"Thank you. Thank you for staying with me."

"Let me know if you need anything?"

"I will."

"This too will get better," Sloane assured. "I know you don't believe it now, but time will prove me right. Trust it. Trust yourself."

"Thank you."

Thandy clicked the line closed, turned off the ringer, and struggled to get some sleep. Sloane was the big brother she never had. She hadn't slept more than a few minutes at a time since the night she lost the baby. In another time, another place, she would have prayed for nothing more precious. But now, long after the dam broke, she could imagine no greater blessing than losing it. "In every blessing there is a curse, a curse in every blessing," Cump would say.

Two hours later, Montana woke her with a glass of orange juice and the morning *Sun-Times*. Thandy sat up and drank nearly half the glass in a single gulp.

"There's a call for you," she said, handing her mother the cordless phone.

"What time is it?" Thandy said as she unfolded the paper.

"Seven."

"Who would be calling me at seven in the morning?"

"He says his name is Jack."

Chapter 17

Yvetta and Grace had next to nothing to say to each other for the better part of two months. Yvetta was still smarting over Grace's history lesson. She didn't need anybody to remind her that her daughter hadn't been home and that she'd been too stubborn to drive up to Chicago to see about her. One would nod politely to the other if they met in line at the grocery store, although generally Grace and Yvetta avoided each other. Jesse Fields told Yvetta how silly it all seemed.

"Go on about your business, Fields. This ain't your row to hoe."

She hid behind her newspaper, hoping he'd vanish, but Fields kept talking. He snapped the straps on his bib overalls and said, "I see Holder has been around here. You ain't thinking about paying him no money to handle that tree, are you?"

"What business is that of yours?" she said from behind the sports section she was pretending to read.

"None, I reckon," he said from the other side of the chain-link fence. "I just know he ain't never been no good on nobody's job. Always leaves things half done. I hope you didn't give him any money up front." Fields shrugged his shoulders and walked away.

Now that Trip Holder had two hundred of Yvetta's dollars in his pocket, he was less than enthusiastic about cutting down that tree. He arrived, looked at it up and down, and left earlier that morning. Holder promised to come back around noon, but it was nearing three o'clock in the afternoon and she hadn't heard a word edgewise from him. Fields might have gotten right to it, but Holder had her money now. She'd knock his teeth down his throat if she ever saw him again.

Grace pulled her new white Cadillac into her driveway across the street, looked up at Yvetta sitting on the porch, and went inside her house. A short time later, Grace emerged in work gloves and a head scarf. She pulled weeds from the edge of the drive. Every once in a while she would steal a glance across the road. Yvetta noticed but ignored her and continued to read the paper. The air was cool. Grace went into her house and came back with a brown, hand-knitted button-down sweater. It was Yvetta's and she'd borrowed it two winters back. Returning it today was as good of an excuse as any to go on across the street. She got as far as the gatepost when Yvetta saw her coming and got up to go in the house.

"I just want to give you your sweater back," Grace called from Fields's favorite spot on the concrete walkway.

"You've had it this long. Another winter won't hurt," Yvetta threw out.

"Yvetta Malone, you come on out here and get this sweater."

Yvetta turned around and looked curiously at Grace.

"We'll be neighbors for the rest of our lives, Yvetta. We can't keep this up forever."

"Suit yourself," she said as she descended the stairs.

She joined Grace at the gate. Both gave short apologies and Yvetta invited Grace in for coffee.

"I could use a cup. Word around here is Trip Holder ran off with your money."

"That don't make it so. You want some sweet rolls?"

"Cinnamon?"

"You know it."

Yvetta cut two thick slices and put them on the good plates.

"That tree is still leaning out back. One good wind and it'll be laying across this kitchen," Grace said as she mashed her fork into the soft brown cake. "Jesse says you gave him money up front."

"Jesse Fields talks too much. He don't know nothing about me or my money."

"I can send my nephew Ronnie Lee around there to get it back, if you want."

"I'll see after Holder. He ain't crazy enough to run off with my money."

"You just let me know and I'll send him on around there. If he puts up a fuss, Ronnie Lee'll tan his behind."

"No sense in that."

"You should ask Fields to see about it for you."

"The tree or the money?"

"Both. I reckon he'll do just about anything for you, if you let him."

"You know how I feel about menfolk in my house."

"We're just talking about your yard, Vetta."

"I know."

"You're sweet on him, aren't you?"

Yvetta blushed. It had been a long time since a man came calling like Fields did. Simon used to wait for her at the edge of the school yard every day until she let him walk her home.

"I ain't sweet on nobody."

"You can tell that lie to somebody else. This here is Grace Goins you're talking to. I've known you for forty-some-odd years. You're about as sweet as the icing on this here pan of rolls about that man."

"You don't know everything. I ain't got no eyes for that old cooter."

"I know the smell of love when I see it."

"Hush yourself."

"You hush yourself. Yvetta, we were lucky enough to find decent men who loved us no end. To find it twice is a blessing. You can't keep throwing God's blessings away."

Yvetta grew silent. She was thinking about how nice it would be to have Fields over for dinner one evening. She'd slow cook a big pot a beef stew and bake a pan of cornbread. He'd eat every bit of it while she watched. Jesse Fields was a large, brown man just like her Simon. He had strong hands and big shoulders. After his wife, Sadie, passed on ten years back, he retired from the Michelin tire plant over near Charlotte and moved back to Winston-Salem. They didn't have any children and Jesse thought it might be nice to live closer to his brother Johnny. It wasn't long before Johnny passed on, too.

Fields had been enamored with Yvetta since he returned to Winston-Salem. Dressed in overalls, a flannel shirt, and work boots, Fields would come to Yvetta's at first light every Saturday. Without fail, the object of his affection would be sitting on the front stoop reading the morning paper. She wanted to think he was just being nice, but he came by even when she treated him bad and left him standing on the sidewalk talking to nobody but himself. He'd look up at the sky and turn on back home.

He lived alone, just three blocks from Yvetta, in a neatly kept brick ranch with perfectly trimmed hedges and white shutters that he painted every spring. Sometimes, he'd see her in town at Drake's Hardware and ask her about the tree or anything else that might need doing. She was generally polite, but mildly disinterested. Armenious Drake watched them avoid shopping on the same aisle until they'd meet at the cash register. Yvetta was occasionally short a few dollars and Drake would wave her on. Fields always picked up the tab.

Grace and Yvetta had just finished their second cups, talked politics like experts, and quickly decided that Sloane Faulkner, the newly elected governor, was something just short of a messiah. The mailman came making rounds just as they were anointing Faulkner Savior of All Things Colored. Yvetta leaned over and watched the mailman through the screen door, then got up and went outside. It was 3:00 p.m. on the nose. At least he was on time. Yvetta met the carrier at the gate and took hold of the thin stack of letters. The big yellow envelope announced in bold black letters that she may have already won twenty-six million dollars. She smiled slightly and threw it in the garbage can at the top of the driveway. She never remembered getting anything for free any day in her life.

You don't always get what you pay for, but you always pay for what you get, she sighed.

Trip Holder pulled his heap of a truck up in the drive a short time later and got his chain saw and some rope out of the back. She escorted him to the tree and left him to his own devices. She went back to the stoop and slipped on her dime-store reading glasses. She opened a pretty beige envelope that had a Chicago postmark. The Serenity Prayer was printed on the front of the card. Inside, Thandy's handwriting read,

> *Dear Mother, We are in Chicago and doing well. I have a new job and a new house. I hope you will visit soon. Love, Thandy.*

She closed the card, said "*Thank you, Jesus,*" forgot the rest of the mail, and went into the house.

"Did the mailman bring anything good today?" Grace snooped.

"Just a stack of bills I can't pay. Ed McMahon's got a big check for me. He oughta be around here with some balloons and roses after a while."

She slipped the card into her apron and sat down at the kitchen table. Grace knew her friend had something on her mind. The sound of the buzzing chain saw cranked up until the women could barely hear one another.

"What are you thinking about?" Grace yelled with her fingers in her ears.

"I ain't studying nothing."

"Are you sure? I can see the smoke billowing out of your head."

The sawing stopped.

"If you must know, I'm thinking about going to see my grandbaby."

"It's been a while since you got over to Charlotte."

"I'm thinking about going to Chicago."

Grace smiled. They heard a crash come from the backyard and Holder was yelling. The women ran out the rear door and found him pinned under the tree. The trunk missed him, but a spread of branches had him nailed to the ground.

"Lord, Jesus, Yvetta," Grace said, almost laughing. "Get on the phone and call Jesse Fields."

"I don't have his phone number."

"Look it up. It's in the book."

Yvetta shook her head, went back inside, got out a phone book, and called Fields. He was at her door ten minutes later.

Chapter 18

Dr. Whitehead pushed his chair back from the desk and said, "That's not her."

"What do you mean, that's not her?"

"That's not the woman who came to my office," Whitehead said, shaking his head. "She's a stone cold fox. That's for sure. But that's not her."

"And you're sure about that, Whitey?"

"I've never been so sure about anything in my entire life. That's not the woman who came to my office. They're both mighty fine."

Jack put the photo of a bikini-clad Angel in his breast coat pocket. Whitehead stood up, took off his lab coat, and hung it on a hook on the back of his door.

"She almost got away with this," he said, sighing deeply. He rubbed both eyes with his thumbs. "I've got to admit, she had a good game going."

"What made you question it?"

"She could've very well been pregnant and it wouldn't have been anybody's fault but mine."

"You should bottle that and sell it."

Whitehead pulled off his tie.

"Sell what?"

"That sixth sense thing."

"Funny, I don't feel like I got a piece of sense in my head. I do know one thing. I'm going to call the curtain on this one."

An hour later, sitting on his living room sofa with his legs comfortably propped up on the coffee table, Jack phoned Angel. She picked up on the first ring and he invited her to dinner.

"It's time we talked about the future," he smiled at the handset, fighting to contain his glee. "I'll pick you up at seven-thirty."

Angel nearly tripped over the phone cord and raced to the shower. She frantically searched her closet for a black cocktail dress and strapped high heels. It would be a cool night out, but she knew Jack adored the sight of well-manicured toes. She emptied out the previous night's tips and went to the nail salon. She was in a hurry, she explained.

"Red! You do red," Ming Lei, her favorite attendant, said. "Your doctor friend will love red. Red say passion," she giggled.

Angel sat back in the spa chair and fantasized about going to a fancy restaurant as the nail techs continued to giggle and chatted in some unintelligible language. She quickly decided that her dress wasn't good enough, so she stopped by a boutique on the way home and bought an off-the-rack, never-say-die strapless for good measure, draining three hundred dollars from her debit card. She spent the next few hours washing and flat ironing her hair until it was bone straight. At precisely 7:00 p.m., she slipped on the new dress and strapped on her shoes. She lit a few candles, turned on some soft music, and waited impatiently for Jack's arrival. Her girlfriend Stephanie called. Angel hastily explained the situation.

"He's taking you to a restaurant?"

"Yeah girl, isn't that great!"

"His divorce isn't final yet?"

"No, but it won't be long."

"How did he sound when you told him you were pregnant?"

"He wasn't happy at first."

"At first?"

"Well, he still isn't fond of the idea."

"Are you sure he won't find out it was me?"

"Whitehead wouldn't know me from a hole in the ground. By the time Jack figures it out, I'll be on my honeymoon," Angel said with confidence.

"How are you going to play pregnant?"

"I'm not. Just give me a few weeks. I stopped taking those damn pills before we went to Barbados. I'll be pregnant before you know it."

"Girl, he can count. He's a doctor."

"He's still a man," she said, checking her reflection. "Like I said, before he figures anything out I'll be a very pregnant Mrs. Gabrielle."

"Where is he taking you for dinner?"

"Some place called Angelo's."

"That's way up in Alpharetta! I hope you know what you're doing."

"I'll send you a postcard from Anguilla."

She said good-bye and quickly hung up when the doorbell rang. Angel straightened her dress, checked her makeup in the foyer mirror, and opened the door.

"Hey you," she cooed as she invited him inside.

"Hey you, yourself," he lathered.

He waited on the sofa as she sashayed around the house blowing out the candles. He lifted an eyebrow and settled in for the show.

The drive to the restaurant was long and mostly silent. Angel tried to stir up some small talk, but Jack mostly just nodded, smiled, and kept driving. He didn't say much more even after they arrived. They studied the menus and said little. When dinner arrived, Angel told him how nice she thought the restaurant was. She had ordered the duck; Jack frowned slightly at her plate. Angel looked up, twisted a half grin, and dug in.

By the time dessert arrived, Jack realized the clock was running out. He wanted to avoid a scene and thought surely she would mind her manners in public. But Angel was chewing her food like a racehorse. He'd chosen an out-of-the-way place— somewhere no one would know him. He was pleased with that now. He took a long pull on a flute of Prosecco and said finally, "I guess we have something to talk about." Before she opened her mouth, Jack went on, "I cannot father another child."

She suddenly stopped eating and looked away.

"I'll be fifty in a few years and I just didn't plan to spend my retirement that way. I'm sorry."

The waiter came by and refilled their water glasses.

"Besides, you don't want to raise a child alone. All the child support money in the world won't make it easy. I've got to be honest with you. I can't give you the big picture. You're a nice girl and all, but you deserve somebody who can give you what you need."

He almost sounded like her father. Jack was nearly twenty years her senior, a fact that wasn't lost on him. He studied her face for a moment. She was very pretty, if not naive. He regretted leading her on, but she was a big girl, he reasoned. If she was big enough to play the game, she was big enough to get played.

"Of course, it wouldn't be easy," she said. "You do love me, don't you, Jack?"

"I'm sorry. I know this hurts you."

The clock stopped moving.

"Angel, you're a nice girl and we had a good time. The truth is I never wanted it to be more than that."

Neither took a breath for the next ten seconds.

"Let's get something straight," she said, sitting up in her chair. "I am pregnant and this is your baby. I am going to have this child with you or without you. Now I understand perfectly the need to keep things quiet. But your divorce is in the works and I'll keep my mouth shut until it's over."

Jack shook his head and tried to beat off the anger. "Please, keep your voice down."

He wanted to wrap his hands around her precious little

throat. His head was running laps around the table. The romance had begun in the backseat of his 7 Series BMW the first night they met. The wheels came off a few months later when she started calling him at the office. Every message was marked urgent. After a bit of cajoling, Angel agreed to let things cool off. When the National Physician's Association convened their annual meeting in Barbados, Jack didn't see any harm in taking Angel along. Thandy, after all, seemed to be engrossed in her work. And when she wasn't in her own office, she was licking stamps for Sloane's campaign. Jack filled out the conference registration package and put down Angel's name under spouse.

"We should talk about the future," Angel said.

"I thought I made that clear."

"And I am very clear. I'm having this child. Your child."

Jack cleared his throat. "Let me guess. You want money."

"Don't be silly. I don't want your money."

"Well, I'll be damned. You'd be by yourself."

"I just want our baby to have both of his parents."

"You should grow up," he fumed.

"You told me you wanted to get married. Remember in Barbados?"

Jack remembered perfectly. He'd said enough to grease her skin and slide her out of her bikini. He said something about getting married and her bathing suit magically fell off. He hadn't meant a word of it. If he ever found himself standing on his own two legs in a church again, reciting vows of marriage, it would be with Thandy.

"Yeah, I remember. That's when I thought you were more responsible."

"I'm not the only one *responsible* for this. You're the one who likes going in bare ass!" she said just as the waiter approached the table. "They still make condoms, you know."

Unashamed, Angel kept talking until the entire restaurant could hear her.

"I said keep your voice down," he sneered.

"Or what, Jack? Keep my voice down or you'll do what?"

He reached for his wallet and threw three one-hundred-dollar bills on the table. Two for dinner, the third for Angel's tirade.

"It's time to go," he said, yanking her up by the arm.

"Let go of me!" she snatched back.

Everyone in the room stopped and watched like they would any good train wreck. Jack pulled her from the table and escorted her to the car.

"You think you can just shove me around like this? Take your hands off me!" she demanded.

"Get in the car!"

"I'm not going anywhere with you."

"I said get your ass in the goddamned car!"

She swung her fist and he caught her by the wrist.

"You better think long and hard before you swing on me," he said, gripping her by both wrists.

She bit him on the knuckle. Angel then hawked up a mouth full of phlegm and spit in his face. His open hand went all the way to China and came back with a terrible force to her face. Angel dropped like a rock.

"I said, get in the car!" he ordered.

Angel crawled inside, sobbing. He picked up her shoe from the pavement and tossed it in after her, barely missing her head.

"Do not think for two seconds that you will ever, ever tell me what I will and won't do!" he started as he wiped the saliva from his nose with his breast scarf. "I don't do ultimatums. I'm telling you right here, right now, we are finished. And by the way, you're not pregnant. I don't know who went to Dr. Whitehead's office, but it wasn't you."

His eyes were on fire, lit up like a pair of tiki torches. He loosened his tie with one hand and steered with the other. The car jerked and blazed forward. She cowered in the passenger seat, holding her face as he tore out of the parking lot.

"I swear, I swear before God that if you ever spit in my face again, you'll regret it for the rest of your pitiful life. Since you're off in La La Land and can't seem to think straight, I'll do it for you. Do you know how many women want to be Mrs. Gabrielle? Shit, the current Mrs. Gabrielle still wants the job! And you thought you could pretend to be pregnant and *poof*, all of your lovely little wishes would come true?"

He punched the accelerator and tore through the streets.

"Jack! Slow down!"

He blew right through the tollbooth express lane.

"Shut your mouth, Angel. For once, just shut your fucking mouth. You talk too fucking much!"

Twenty minutes later he pulled up to the curb in front of her house and told her to get out.

She didn't move at first.

"Bitch, get out of my car."

She reached for the door handle and said, "I don't want you to be angry with me. I can explain."

"Well, yeah, that's what you say."

Before she could get her feet planted on the sidewalk, he reached over, slammed the door and sped away.

"Damn lunatic," he muttered.

Chapter 19

The house was dark and quiet. Jack stopped in the kitchen first for a snap of cognac, then went down to the cellar. The first shot made him forget all about Angel. The next made him remember Thandy.

He'd called her that morning. Her voice was soft and somewhat distant. He did most of the talking. Jack was just glad she was listening; he wanted her to hear him. He'd only summoned the nerve to call her after Sloane told him that he had spoken to her. He wanted to hear her say Chicago was a mistake and that she was coming home on the next flight out. That she still loved him and wanted nothing more than their life together. He might have waited for a more decent hour, but he couldn't bring himself to let another minute go by.

"We've filed for divorce," he had explained.

"And?" Thandy said.

"And it's almost over. I don't want things to drag out, so I'm going to settle."

"Good," she had said softly. "That's the best thing for your sons."

"Thandy, I want to come up to see you."

"It's not a good time," she told him.

"You've got a lot on your shoulders. It sounds like a great opportunity. I don't want to rush anything."

"There's nothing to rush," she whispered.

"Listen, baby. I'm trying to say I'm sorry. I wish we were having this conversation in person. Hell, I didn't even know where to find you. Sloane wouldn't even give me your number at first." He'd paused. "You just took off."

Thandy said nothing.

"How is Chicago treating you?" Jack said with a softer tone.

"It's fine. It's a little chilly for November, but otherwise fine. We've had a few light flurries, but I hear the worst is yet to come."

"I hope it snows like hell."

"I love snow, Jack. When I was little girl it would snow up to the front doorstep every January. It's my favorite time of year. My grandfather used to call me his January girl. Listen, Jack. It was good to hear from you. And I hope things turn out the way you want them to."

She was trying to say good-bye, but he had more to say.

"You're more like an October surprise. We had an anniversary last month," he reminded her as he tossed his feet onto the carpet and got out of bed.

"I thought you might have forgotten."

"How could I? I've had ten years with the most wonderful woman alive."

"You never remembered before."

"I'm sorry, Thandy. I was selfish."

"I never asked for a lot. I never asked you to be or do anything."

"That's the most wonderful thing about you. I want to make it up to you if you'll let me."

"I'm not sure you can."

"So, is this good-bye?"

She'd paused and said, "Indeed."

He could hear the quake in her voice. Jack wanted right then to put his arms around her, to kiss away every disappointment he'd given her. But she was five hundred miles away, sufficiently out of reach.

"I wish I could say something to change your mind," he'd said. "I just want you to have the best of everything."

"Then let me go."

As he leaned back in the nursing chair, he played their conversation again and again. The cognac that usually steadied him had made it to his brain and was loosening his muscles. He started to count to ten, then started over again. His breathing slowed and his legs steadied. There was a rumbling on the floor above his head.

"Dr. Gabrielle, it's the police!"

Jesus, he thought. *That bitch.*

Flora Perez, the housekeeper, had opened the door. She pointed them to the cellar. Jack thought quickly as he heard the officers descend the stairs. He put his hands in the air.

"I'm unarmed," Jack called across the room.

They followed Jack upstairs to the living room, where he was ordered to sit on the sofa. One officer questioned the housekeeper briefly, then released her.

"Lo siento, Dr. Gabrielle," she said as she went upstairs. "I am sorry."

"Toda será multa, everything will be fine."

Afraid the authorities would discover she was in the country illegally, she went straight to her room and packed her clothes.

"Dr. Gabrielle, did you have dinner with a Miss Angel Delafine?" one of the officers asked, hovering over him.

"Delafuenta," he corrected. "I did. I took her to Angelo's on Alpharetta Highway."

"You argued with her there?"

"She did most of the talking," Jack said, looking away.

"Is it fair to say you had a disagreement?"

"You could say that. She was screaming like a crazy woman. The whole restaurant heard it. There must have been a hundred people there."

"Did you strike Miss Delafuenta? She said you threatened her life."

"I need to call my lawyer."

Jack took the cordless phone into the kitchen and dialed Parham. The lawyer appeared at the front door less than fifteen minutes later. He greeted the officers and motioned Jack to join him in the den.

"What's this about?" Parham whispered as he closed the double French doors.

"Some girl says I hit her."

"Did you?"

Jack said nothing.

"Did you?"

"Yeah," he whispered. "Only after she swung on me and spit in my face. Look at this shit!" Jack held up his bloody knuckle. "She bit me."

"Who is she?"

"Her name is Angel."

"Are you fucking *her*, too?"

"I was. But then she lied and told me she was pregnant."

"Ah, man, you're smarter than that. If Etienne gets wind of this, you can kiss your whole damn kingdom good-bye."

"She's not pregnant. Manipulative, but not pregnant."

"That doesn't matter. It's another affair, my man. Etienne will unload all of this in court. You got anything else you need to tell me?"

"No, that's it."

"If I'm going to get you out of this mess, you'll have to come straight with me," Parham pressed, standing between Jack and the door. "We're not going back out there until you tell me everything. I can't defend you if you're going to keep coming up with surprises."

"That's it," he lied again. Now wasn't the time to unearth a decade of indiscretions. The others were irrelevant—vestiges of the well-staged life he was no longer drawn to.

The men walked back to the living room where Jack calmly answered a barrage of questions. He was suddenly sure of himself again. Parham's presence stiffened his back. There were two of them and now the score was even.

"My client was only acting in self-defense," Parham advised. "The woman in question attacked him first."

"She admits that, but she's got one heck of a shiner," the taller, thinner officer said. "She says you wouldn't let her out of the car. She's claiming false imprisonment."

"We were all the way up in Alpharetta. That's at least twenty-five miles north. What was I supposed to do? Put her out on Georgia 400? Drop her off at the tollbooth?" Jack explained. "I took her straight home. It was late."

"The law says we have to book you both. The judge will have to sort this out."

The officers cuffed Jack and took him to a waiting squad car. Parham followed the cruiser to the station house. The next morning, after he posted a cash bond, Jack instructed Parham to approve the settlement. Etienne got everything she wanted. Angel sat in jail for four days until her mother could wire the bail money. Two weeks later, after a round of negotiation, Jack and Angel stood before a judge and dropped the charges.

Chapter 20

It was just after 8:00 a.m. Two lawyers and three accountants sat around the conference table, their ties already down at half-mast, their sleeves already rolled up when Etienne came in. Every man there, including Wynn Finlayson, had been summoned—her very own handpicked team of experts. There were decisions to be made and a ton of money to count.

One by one, as if on cue, the men carefully laid out the matters at hand. Jack Gabrielle had rolled over like a patsy. Etienne would have enjoyed it better if he'd begged. He could kiss her ass until the sun came up and it wouldn't make a difference. For her part, Etienne started counting wins the old-fashioned way, a dollar at a time. She had fifteen million reasons to be happy.

"I find it hard to believe he just gave in like that," she said, snapping her fingers. "The Jack Gabrielle I know hates to lose."

"I was a little surprised myself," Finlayson said.

Etienne smiled with sweet satisfaction and nodded to a far-off place.

"Seems everything runs its course," she said to no one, hardly able to contain her glee.

"These things have a way of working themselves out," Finlayson said. "The point is you got everything there was to get. No jury trial."

"Are we sure about that?"

"If he has any other assets, then he's done a mighty fine job of hiding them."

"I don't put anything past him. I trust him about as far as I can pick him up and throw him."

"I thought you might toss him out of a window," Finlayson laughed.

"The day isn't over yet," she grinned.

The first accountant took the cue and began detailing the settlement ad nauseam. He spoke in clear, short sentences like every other CPA on the planet. He was compulsive, if not anal retentive, relishing every detail. Etienne liked the idea that the team was so thorough, although she couldn't muster the concentration to follow along for more than a few minutes at a time. She wanted them to spare the gory details. Jack had always managed the family finances, something she regretted now. Most of the information was news to her. How much was here, how much was there. Etienne was soon bored and began to fidget after the first hour.

A second lawyer presented her with the settlement documents. Etienne scanned the paperwork. The actual court date was many weeks away, but technically she was a free woman—a very rich and very free woman. Staring away again to some far-off place, she hardly heard a word of their briefing. She cared only about one number: fifteen. At that moment she wandered upon a frightening thought. She had no husband, no house to go home to. She didn't even own a car. Etienne hadn't planned for the day after. She'd gotten by on Jack's American Express Black Card and a hired town car.

The lawyers had been up well past midnight preparing for her arrival, anticipating any questions she would have, but instead Etienne picked sparingly at her muffin. Orange-cranberry, no sugar, just as she requested.

"I can't say I know what I'm doing," she said finally. "It's not like I get divorced every day."

"Take your time," Finlayson instructed. "Make sure you understand everything."

She skimmed through the paragraphs and initialed the changes. She blew out a lengthy sigh, then signed and dated the last page. One of the accountants signed as a witness and then the notary added her seal, after which the stack was ferried off to the copier.

"I don't even know where to start," she said as she stood up from the long table. "I think I need a car."

"You've got enough money to start over any way you want," Finlayson said.

"I don't know what I want."

"It'll come to you."

His voice was steady and sure, comforting. When she was satisfied, Etienne pushed back from the table and stood up.

"I should get going."

"I imagine you've already set up an account to receive the funds."

"I hadn't thought about it really," she said. "I'm ashamed to say I've never had a bank account of my own. I've been living on Jack's credit card since the day I left."

"You should open your own account. After the judge signs the final order, you'll need to be ready to receive the funds. You'll need a solid financial strategy. And don't spend any more money until you decide what you really want. The order makes you personally responsible for any new debt incurred after the day you left."

"Any recommendations?"

"I have a colleague who runs the Wealth Management practice at a big firm. They're out of Chicago, but they've got a great reputation," one of the accountants offered. "The division president is from Atlanta. I think you will like her."

"Thandy Malone," Etienne guessed.

Her cool, methodical tone evaporated. According to Etienne's calculations, Thandy Malone had been in Chicago several months. Her phone call had hit the mark. Still, just the thought of her name caused a violent eruption in Etienne.

Even still, she tried to tell herself she didn't have bad feelings for Thandy, that she was just one of Jack's more than frequent infidelities. *Bitches and whores.* She tried to tell herself that Thandy was as common as the rest. The revelation that Jack had been seeing her for ten years fell on Etienne's head like an avalanche of bricks. She could live with the idea that her husband was fucking a string of women as casually as he changed his underwear. But not that he spent years with one woman.

She didn't even have her own bank account. How had she been so stupid?

"You know her?" the accountant asked.

Before Finlayson could stop her, she said, "She's my husband's mistress. Ex-husband," she corrected. "I guess now she's his ex-mistress."

"I'm sorry. I didn't know," he said, sliding down into his seat. "I'm sure there's another firm."

"If she's really smart, she'll forget him," Etienne said.

"I'll compile a list of good firms," Finlayson tossed out, trying to change the subject.

Unfortunately, Etienne was already caught up in yesterday. Finlayson walked her to the elevator and left her with a strong hug as the door opened.

"I just want to say thank you, Finny. I know he's your friend."

"I guess he won't be speaking to me after this."

"He isn't the kind to forgive easily, but he'll come around."

"Maybe."

"In the meantime, sell the condo. How much did you say it was worth?"

"Two million flat, sight unseen. It's yours. You can move in."

"Not a chance. Sell it. Give Liddy my best."

"Will do."

The elevator door closed. Etienne smiled broadly as she descended the floors. The strong scent of the rain-soaked city filled her nose as she stepped out of the revolving door. The black town car was waiting at the curb.

"Where to, Mrs. Gabrielle?"

"Ms. Pulliam," she quickly corrected. "Head out 20 west and then take 285 south to the Cascade Road exit."

She needed to see the boys, to be with them, to hold them. She parceled out a few drippings of small talk as the town car moved swiftly through the streets and up the on-ramp. The driver nodded, but said nothing.

Her mind raced back to their first Christmas together. Jack promised twelve days of Christmas splendor. Instead, he showed up wearing a Santa hat and carrying a gift bag, undoubtedly bought at a dime store. She remembered how excited she was to open it. Inside was a bottle of disappointment wrapped in tissue paper. No offense to Mary Kay, but given that her darling Jack was a trust-fund baby and well on his way to a storied career in neurology, she found the gift cheap and thoughtless. Still she smiled.

The next day, presumably in keeping with the second day of Christmas, he brought another gift. More Mary Kay. Maybe he was climbing up to something, but he was out of rope. Even though she wanted to strangle him with that rope, Etienne expressed her discontent in the kindest way she could. He promised to do better. They made love that night and every night after that for ten days. His tidings grew marginally better. But when she discovered another girl's phone number in his clinical jacket, Etienne blew her top. They spent the remainder of the holiday season apart. When they did get back together, he expected that they would just pick up where they left off. He never apologized.

She wished now that she had been smart enough, strong enough to walk away then. Over the years, there had been so many indiscretions, so many late nights and strangely private cell phone calls, that she simply lost count.

Gail and the boys were waiting on the stoop when the car pulled up to the curb. They ran out to meet their mother.

"Mama! Mama!" they called.

They ran as fast as their little brown legs could carry them. They'd seen her only two or three times in the last few weeks. She didn't want them to see her in pain. She'd already told them about the divorce, though she was sure Jacob didn't know what it meant at the time.

"We're getting a new house," she told them as they hugged her waist.

"I like Auntie Gail's house," Jack Jr. announced.

"You can pick any house you want," she told him.

"I want to go home," Jacob said, confused.

"Baby," she said, kneeling down until her eyes met his. "Remember what Mama said? Mama and Daddy are going to live in different houses from now on."

"He's not going to the new house with us?"

"No, baby. But you can go see him anytime you want."

"How come he hasn't come yet?" Jack asked. "Auntie Gail said he would come, but he didn't."

"He's been very busy."

"Can we call him?"

"Sure, baby. You can call him."

"I wanna call him now," Jacob pleaded. "Right now, Mom."

"Not right now, baby." Etienne's eyes welled up with tears.

"How come we can't call him right now, Mama?" Jacob said, tugging her skirt.

"Baby, Daddy is in surgery. He's working at the hospital," she said, telling the first lie that came to mind. She didn't really know where Jack was. Until the boys asked, she didn't really care.

"C'mon fellas," Gail said. "Let's get your things."

Gail took the boys by the hands and led them back into the house. She turned to Etienne and said, "It gets better, girl."

Etienne looked up at the sky. The clouds were starting to clear. She hadn't taken a drink in several months, not since the plane ride home to D.C., and she was pleased with herself.

Chapter 21

Thandy stared at the roses on her credenza. She picked up the phone and dialed Phillipa.

"He called you? What could he possibly want?" Phillipa asked.

"I'm not sure."

"What do you mean you're not sure?" Phillipa pressed. "Girl, don't you dare think about giving in. You've come too damn far for that."

"He sent roses. They got here a few days ago."

"So what? He sent some damn roses. Don't tell me this is the first time he ever sent roses. He's still the same Jack Gabrielle. Ain't nothing changed about that. He probably ordered them from QuikTrip. Did they throw in a free slushy?"

"I've been through a lot," Thandy conceded.

"Don't let a bunch of roses make you forget that. Nothing and I mean nothing trumps the pain and neglect he laid at your doorstep. Remember, you were in that hospital room by yourself."

"I gave him back the house."

"You did what?"

"And the car."

"You're nuts."

"I don't need it. I don't need him. I can afford my own stuff. I've got a wonderful life, Philly. I won't give that up. I don't need some broke-back prince to save me from anything."

"That's my girl. But I still would've kept the house. You could've gave me the car."

Thandy assured her friend that she was just fine, and said, "Listen, I've got to run. I've a got a full docket today."

"Do yourself a favor."

"Yes?"

"Don't take his calls. Throw the flowers away and move on, baby. Move on. You don't want what he's selling."

Thandy laid the phone down on the receiver and pushed herself back from her desk.

The conference room was full when Thandy walked in. She took her seat at the head of the table and opened the agenda.

"Good morning, ladies and gentlemen."

There was ample cause for anxiety. The last few quarters had been decidedly less than stellar, despite the addition of several new accounts. Thandy quickly got to the point.

"Bad margins," she said. "We're extending far too much effort. The accounts are overstaffed."

"What are you suggesting?" Stafford asked.

"I'm not suggesting anything. The point is we're billing too much in senior hours. Some of the work should be shifted to the middle team. I expect the solutions to come from each of you. You've got three days to hammer out a better allocation of talent. I expect some of the smaller clients to be shifted to the retail side of the house."

"That's at least thirty percent of the client base," Roberto Cervante jumped in. "That'll shrink our revenues and we won't make our numbers."

"Most of the people in this room aren't making their numbers now," she countered.

Cervante shrank away.

"We," she continued, "haven't made our numbers for three quarters and counting. The year-over-year is dismal and I'm giving you one more quarter to straighten it out. Two to show some results," she said flatly. "If we shift the thirty to discount retail that will free up senior counsel to pitch and win a new bank of business. We'll need to establish stronger criteria. Goldman requires a ten million dollar minimum."

"We're not Goldman," Stafford piped in.

"And we never will be if we don't start acting like it," Thandy dismissed. "What I am saying is that if we keep positioning ourselves at the bottom of the market then that's where we will stay. We're not a discount house, but we're acting like one. Ten million is a strong number. We'll have to set the right number for us. Everything is about positioning."

The room was silent.

"I will say this," Thandy added. "The T&E budget is way out of line."

She opened a manila folder and handed out a summary report of the quarter's expenses. Each executive's submitted and paid expenses were calculated against the related account. Those that fell over twenty-five percent were highlighted in yellow. Those over thirty percent were in red. Cervante's name was at the top. His travel and expense rang in at thirty-six percent.

"For some of you, especially those in red, I expect some immediate action. I want you to think twice before you sign your name to an expense report. Ultimately, I will hold you accountable for how you spend our clients' money."

Thandy ran through a housekeeping list. Among the items was a planned competitive bid for the firm's technology infrastructure implementation and IT services.

"We'll release the Request of Proposal late next week."

She went on to establish a standing leadership team meeting each Monday at 7:00 a.m.

"If you're traveling, I expect you to dial in. The meeting will last one hour. Block your calendar. Bring your weekly financials.

Top-line only. The count will run from Saturday to Saturday. I expect a soft copy via e-mail every Sunday before 4:00 p.m. I will accept no excuses, so don't keep me waiting. If you suspect your line of business won't make the stated targets, tell me about that in the body of the e-mail. Do not surprise me. I hate surprises. Manage my expectations, ladies and gentlemen."

She stood up and adjourned the meeting. The group was afraid to move.

"Cervante, meet me in my office," she directed.

"I have a client conference call in ten minutes," he returned.

"With whom?"

"George Overstreet. He's set to pull the trigger on fifty million in assets."

"Stafford, what do you have on your plate?" she said, turning to John.

"I'm flying to New York to see TriVest."

"Can you get a later flight?"

He hesitated. "Sure, if necessary."

"It's necessary. I want you to staff the Overstreet call."

The blood rushed from Cervante's face. He pushed in his chair and nodded to Stafford. Thandy left the conference room and he followed like a dead man walking. She went into her office, waved Cervante in, and closed the door behind them.

"Take a seat." She walked over to the windowsill and started talking to the glass. "You've been with the firm over five years."

"Yes."

"And in five years, you've made your bonus target every quarter."

"Yes."

"Somehow, you've made your bonus target but your margins are as thin as tissue paper. When the bottom fell out of the market last year, you maintained your numbers. Oil prices went into the stratosphere and you made your numbers. Hurricane Katrina took out most of the southern coast and sank a whole American city and you made your numbers. Hurricane Rita stopped oil production for a week and you made your numbers. The Dow lost four hundred points and unemployment hit a ten-year high and you made your numbers. I'd say that is cause for applause."

Thandy walked over to the credenza and pulled a manila folder from a stack. She opened the file, skimmed the top sheet, and handed it to Cervante, who looked like he was sweating bullets.

"I must say you're good," she said with sarcasm.

"I don't understand."

"Sure you do. I asked a forensic accountant to take a look at your numbers. We started with the day you joined the firm," she said, handing him a second page. "I thought I was dealing with a modern-day Superman. You've got just five years under your belt and still you outgunned even John Thain," she said, referring to the former president of Goldman Sachs and newly appointed chief executive of the New York Stock Exchange. "I'd say that's one hell of an achievement. Greenspan takes the interest rate up with no sign of stopping, then retires to Florida; consumer confidence is in the toilet; the housing market is about to pop like a grenade; and you still make your numbers."

Thandy paused and looked curiously at Cervante.

"What is VeriSoft?" she asked.

"A privately held software security firm. One of my best clients."

"Really?"

"Yes, Ms. Malone."

Thandy called her secretary. "Get me Victor Sillers. Tell him to come up."

She clicked the line closed and turned her attention back to Cervante. He was by far the highest-ranking Hispanic in the firm. The son of Peruvian immigrants, he earned an MBA from Stanford and graduated in the top one percent of his class. Cervante had been one of the firm's first-round picks. His performance evaluations during his five-year tenure had been impeccable. He took home an annual bonus that exceeded a half million dollars. His father, Eduardo Cervante, was among the country's most highly regarded financial analysts and specialized in Latin American economic matters. He was the first to predict the telecommunications boom that took over the continent. American cell companies and all the Bells called on him for guidance. Roberto was from good stock.

"You've made quite a name for yourself around here."

"This is the only job I ever wanted," he pushed out.

Sillers knocked and entered. He took the chair next to Cervante, who nervously reached to shake his hand. Sillers kept his hands on his knees and said nothing.

"First, let me be straight with you. This is your last day of service at Campbell-Perkins," Thandy said.

"On what grounds?" he protested. "You can't just let me go."

"I can and I have," she said flatly. "You are frankly a very lucky young man."

"I don't feel lucky."

"You're lucky you're not on a train ride down to Marion. Our investigation revealed several things. First, VeriSoft is a shell company with no known revenues. However, somehow, and if you like you can explain it to a judge, they managed to pay this firm over four million in fees last year alone, taking you over your defined performance targets."

She wasn't finished.

"Then there is the matter of your travel and expense reports. On one occasion you submitted receipts for airline tickets to Amelia Island and a stay at the Ritz-Carlton there. However, your cell records indicate that you never left Chicago. I can count dozens of instances just like it."

Cervante thought quickly.

"I paid for a client's travel. Nothing wrong with that. Standard practice."

"Which client? Certainly not VeriSoft. Frankly, I did not believe the initial report. So I asked Mr. Sillers to take another look. Now what do you suppose he found?"

Cervante shrugged his shoulders as Thandy took another slip of paper from the file.

"We checked with the hotel. Your parents were coincidentally on vacation at the same hotel, at the same time. But more importantly, I found six shadow accounts," Sillers said, peeling through a stack of papers. "All shell companies, with no traceable revenues."

"I admire ambition, Mr. Cervante," Thandy said. "In fact, that's how we all got here. But if nothing else, I hate a liar. And I can't stand a thief."

She sat down at her desk and handed him a page from another file. He hadn't noticed it before. The folder was marked "Cervante Separation."

"This is your separation agreement. I don't expect you to sign it right away. If you're smart, you will retain counsel and review this today. If I don't have a signed copy of the agreement by close of business tomorrow, I will turn everything over to Federal prosecutors. I also expect that you will repay every dime that you stole from this firm. You have ten business days to deliver a certified check for three million dollars. That represents the adjusted bonus amounts and repayment of all nonbusiness expenses. If you do that, we will approach this as an employment issue. If you fail to return the funds, then it will become a criminal issue. It's your call."

Cervante took the agreement and left. He rode the elevator down to his office, where two uniformed security guards were already posted outside. His personal effects were already boxed, taped, and loaded onto a mail cart. His nameplate had already been taken down. His e-mail account, corporate American Express, access to the company intranet, and cell phone had already been cancelled. His assistant wouldn't look him in the eye. The guards escorted him from the building and watched as he drove out of the parking deck.

"Aren't you worried that he'll sue us?" Sillers asked.

"Not in the least. He's looking at twenty years hard time if he doesn't sign and pay us back. Any lawyer worth his salt will tell him to sign it and sell lemonade to pay up if he has to."

"That's a lot of lemons."

"He owes us a lot of money. I'll squeeze it out of him, if it comes to that."

"You were tough," Sillers told Thandy. "I'm glad I wasn't sitting in his seat."

"It's a waste. Clearly, he's a talented young man. You know how much I value diversity. Unfortunately, situations like this make every person of color suspect. Truth is, if Cervante were white, nobody would care. If he were black, this would make the evening news and the cover of *The Wall Street Journal*. Does the name Joe Jett ring a bell?"

"Why are you waiting to press charges? We know he won't come up with the money. He probably spent it all."

"Because I believe in second chances. He's a grown man. He'll figure it out."

"You're better than me," Sillers said.

"If he's as smart as I think he is, he put most of the money away. Hell, if you gave me three million over five years, I'd have at least nine to show for it."

"He's not you."

Thandy smiled.

"Who are we going to get to replace him?"

"That's your job."

"I'll set up some time with the search firm this afternoon."

"Save the money. There are at least four internal candidates we should look at first."

"Like who?"

"Genevieve Anderson is at the top of my list."

"But she's right out of grad school."

"She went to Wharton with four years of wealth management already under her belt. Stafford tells me she single-handedly brought in the William Feurst account. That old man doesn't trust anybody with his money."

"I'll take a look at her performance reviews."

"And take a look at Jason Hill. In fact, I'd like to have dinner with four of them. Anderson, Hill, Spraggins, and Waters."

"That's one hell of a lineup."

"Let's not tell them what this is all about."

"I think they're smart enough to figure it out. How often does the CEO ask some junior team members out to dinner?"

"Just tell them I'm conducting some skip-level meetings to get a better feel for the firm. That's the honest truth. I need to know what was happening under Cervante. Who better to tell me than his people?"

"And what about their managers? Do we leave them in the dark, too?"

"Of course we do. One never knows how long any of them will be around anyway. If I thought they were on point, one of them would be coming to dinner with me."

"Point well taken. But we can't just promote one over their boss's head."

"Of course we can," Thandy assured. "If there's one thing I've learned over the course of my career, anything can happen. Things have a way of working themselves out. I will restructure an entire business unit if I have to, just to make way for the right talent to rise."

"If you're going to start cleaning house, shouldn't you let Mr. Perkins in on the plan?"

"He's already aware."

Stafford knocked and entered.

"I heard the news. The water cooler is churning," Stafford commented.

"We'll call an all-hands meeting this afternoon," Thandy said.

"What are we going to tell them?" Sillers begged to know.

"That we've uncovered some irregularities in our accounts and will be conducting an enterprise-wide review," she instructed.

"That'll scare the living shit out of everybody," Sillers said.

"Good. If any one of them has trumped-up earnings, then we'll put them out to pasture."

"What about the quarter?" Stafford asked.

"Depending on how widespread the issue becomes, we may have to restate earnings," Thandy advised.

She punched the intercom button.

"Yes, Ms. Malone?"

"Recall the leadership team. Send them a dial-in number. We'll convene in fifteen minutes in the Campbell conference room."

"Should I send out for lunch?"

"No time for that. Start drafting an e-mail invitation. We're having an all-hands at 4:00 p.m. Mandatory. And please call Mr. Perkins. Tell him it's urgent."

"Yes, Ms. Malone."

The trio sat around looking at one another. Thandy rested her chin on her balled fists. Stafford spoke up first.

"I know I'm getting ahead of myself, but we've got to tell the Street. Client confidence could sink."

"We'll make an announcement immediately following the all-hands. Every client will get a personal call from his or her account manager before the close of business. We will assure the integrity of their accounts and issue a public statement saying we believe the issue has been contained."

"What about Cervante?" Sillers asked. "Didn't we just send him off with a nondisclosure?"

"I didn't include any language to that effect in the agreement. In exchange for his silence on the matter, we agreed not to prosecute."

"Damn," Stafford said. "Once word leaks that he was the target of the investigation, he won't be able to get a job washing cars."

"We don't fire people," Thandy retorted quickly. "People fire themselves. He was finished the moment he opened that first account. I want to know who let it go unchecked. Besides, washing cars isn't such a bad profession."

The intercom buzzed. "Mr. Perkins on line two, Ms. Malone."

"Mr. Perkins, I hope you don't mind. I have you on speakerphone. John Stafford and Victor Sillers are here with me."

"Good afternoon, gentlemen."

"Good afternoon, sir," they returned in unison.

Sillers sat up straight in his chair as if Perkins could see him.

"As we discussed last evening, we let Roberto Cervante go this morning."

"I want to prosecute," Perkins said.

"Yes, sir. I do understand your position. However, I believe prosecution may reveal holes in our business. Proprietary information could come into the public square. I think it's important to hold out the threat of prosecution in return for repayment."

"It's your call."

"No, sir. This is your firm. Your name is over the door."

"I hired you because I knew I could trust you with these matters."

"I appreciate your confidence, sir."

"Stafford, Sillers, take care of Ms. Malone. I'll be back in Chicago in two hours. What's next?"

"We've called a leadership team meeting. We'll convene in a few minutes if you would like to dial in. Later today, we will host an all-hands meeting to announce the Cervante departure, a broader investigation, and a new bonus structure."

"I don't need to be in the first meeting. That would only deposition you, Ms. Malone. Wealth Management has a solid leader and if they don't know that already, they'll know it today. I'll get there in time for the larger gathering, but I don't expect to make a presentation. I'm just coming to show my support and bring some gravity to the situation."

"Thank you, sir," Thandy said as she clicked the line closed.

A few hours later, after an abbreviated meeting with the senior leadership, Thandy stood before a packed auditorium of employees. Ten phone lines were set up so the field offices could dial in remotely. For the first forty-five minutes, Thandy outlined the issues at hand and the steps she would take to cure them. Perkins sat approvingly in the front row.

"I believe that this incident is the work of maverick fraudulent behavior," she went on. "But let's be clear. If our investigation yields more wrongdoing, I have the ultimate responsibility to root out those accountable. Working here is a privilege that we all enjoy. We are the caretakers of our clients' assets and stewards of the Campbell-Perkins brand. This company was built on trust. To the extent that we can maintain that trust, our very credibility is directly tied to our success."

Joel Perkins started to clap. Soon the entire room joined him. Thandy was relieved. Sillers stepped to the podium and outlined a newly crafted bonus structure. The program relied less on individual performance and more on the top-line revenue growth of the firm. The process was streamlined and interdependent by nature.

"This program is designed to reward individual contributions, as well as group performance," he told the crowd. "Business unit leaders will be held responsible for the success of their teams. Rising tides will lift all boats."

Thandy took the microphone again. "I expect that you have questions. If you do not feel comfortable asking them here in the public square, I have set up an e-mail alias through which you can file them anonymously. In the interest of transparency, my team will condense the questions and I will not only answer personally, but I will publish all answers throughout the firm. You have my commitment that you will receive responses by Friday at noon. The answers will be housed on the company intranet site. By all means, do not limit your questions to these matters. My door is open to you."

The public questions were, as expected, few. That afternoon, several dozen employees made use of the anonymous e-mail offer. Thandy, Stafford, and Sillers worked into the night for several evenings straight.

By the close of business Friday, Thandy was glad the week was over. A courier delivered a certified check for three million dollars and the executed separation agreement from Cervante the Crook. She sat alone in her office, poring through quarterly reports. Sillers was the last to leave.

"Hundred-hour weeks never pay off," he said.

"Tell me about it," she returned.

She could have turned everything over to the district attorney, but she would never forget that somebody had once given *her* a second chance. She hoped Cervante wouldn't waste his. Just after midnight, she made the drive home to Hyde Park.

Chapter 22

Jack was one of only two black men ever admitted to membership at the Piedmont Driving Club. Three years ago, in the spirit of diversity, the board of governors gleefully invited the good doctor and K. Frank Dubartlanden, a local real estate developer, to join its prestigious ranks. K-Dub was a scion of the largest black-owned construction company in the country. The Gabrielles summered with them a few years back on Martha's Vineyard. Sipping beers at the Salty Dog, the men decided they would wage a quiet campaign to integrate Piedmont. Not because they were interested in social progress, but for the prestige and envy it would invoke among others. Jack enjoyed the one-up game. But more than that, he adored winning. At the time, Etienne had been duly pleased with his appointment and quickly ferried the news to anyone within earshot.

Situated on the westerly edge of Piedmont Park, the crown jewel of the city, the club exudes elegance. Founded in 1887, the club has enjoyed a reputation as one of the most exclusive private clubs in the South, and has a long history of entertaining the South's social elite as well as countless notable guests, including American presidents and visiting heads of state. As he was sworn in as a member, Jack recalled the day he stood on the baseball diamond, not more than a few hundred yards away, and stared up at the large white house. "Father, who lives there?"

"No one lives there, son. It's a country club."

"Can we join?"

The elder Dr. Gabrielle ignored the question and picked up a leather glove. "Let's throw a few more. The sun's about to go down."

He didn't like to talk about anything he couldn't have. Harvard was one thing, Piedmont was another. The time was long gone when he thought he should have had a conversation with his son regarding the particulars of race, class, and geography. Jack thought back on that day with delight. He had become more than his father had expected, exceeded the bar, and integrated Piedmont.

The Men's Grill at the Piedmont Driving Club had been reserved for the evening. Not even the service staff would be allowed in. Even the governor-elect's driver was relegated to the parking lot. At Jack's insistence, the poker game had to start promptly at nine o'clock. Not that it mattered. He was late and everybody else assumed he would be. Dressed in the obligatory tie and jacket, Doogie and Sloane drifted around the bar while Elijah set up the playing table. Satisfied that there was more liquor than food, he carefully stacked the chips at each man's station and shuffled the cards with the ease of a Las Vegas dealer. Elijah was an old hand. His long brown fingers elegantly moved across the table. When he was satisfied with his work he turned his attention to the others.

"Can I get you gentlemen anything?" he asked.

"You ain't at work, Mr. E.," Sloane said. "If we need something, then we'll see after it ourselves. Tonight, you're one of the fellas."

Doogie was already drinking and had been since noon, two hours after he told his intended he wasn't ready to get married. By midafternoon, his darling fiancée had his bags packed and loaded on the curb. The nasty little war he had predicted never materialized. He was beginning to think she might even have been relieved. She didn't drop a single tear. Her demeanor was as calm as if he'd only told her he'd be running late for dinner. The fact that she was pregnant seemed inconsequential to her.

"My mama and my mama's mama raised babies on their own," she dismissed. "I don't need a man."

He drained a shot of Jack Daniels and immediately poured another.

"Whoa! Slow down, cowboy," Sloane warned. "We got at least two or three hours of drinking left. You can't go on like that all night."

Doogie filled his mouth with liquor and let it roll down his throat like a ball of fire. His girlfriend was six months pregnant. She wouldn't take his calls.

"What's eating you, boy?" Sloane ribbed.

As if clairvoyant, Elijah shuffled over and laid his hand on Doogie's shoulder.

"This here young man's got woman problems," Elijah said.

"Naw, not Doogie," Sloane laughed. "He's getting married in a month."

"Mr. Governor, this here man's got woman problems. I'll put my last dollar on it."

"You keep your dollar, Mr. Elijah, because I aim to beat you out of it tonight. Listen, here. What Doogie has is a case of cold feet."

Sloane was still laughing. Doogie didn't crack a smile. He swayed like there was a wind blowing. Mr. Elijah grabbed him as he was falling.

"Damn, Doogie, you're drunk," Sloane said.

They led him over to the table and let him catch a moment of comfort in the mahogany high-back leather chair. The rule was nobody could sit down until all the players had arrived. Jack wasn't there, and nothing was unusual about that, but Elijah both made and was now breaking the rule. Doogie slumped over and fell off asleep, his nose buried in a cup holder. He was sound asleep and snoring like a leaf blower when Jack arrived.

"Hey! Don't tell me you got started without me!" he sang as he came through the door.

"Just when you need a doctor, one comes strolling in," Sloane said. "The one we got is down for the count."

"What's going on? What's wrong with Doogie?"

"Ah, he's all right. Just a little heartsick," Sloane said. "And drunk."

"Damn. They get the best of them, don't they?"

Doogie was moaning something unintelligible about a dog, no food, and a rusty nail. He, too, had been one of Elijah's students.

"Come on now, Doogie," Jack said, pulling him off the table. "Never let a woman drive you to drinking."

Doogie slumped again. Jack let him rest his head on the table.

"Just don't throw up," he told him. "The board paid good money for that table. Straight from Monte Carlo and cost us five grand. What's he been drinking? Did he eat anything?"

"Jack Daniels," Elijah said. "From the looks of it, I don't think he's got anything in his stomach but that."

"Good. That means nothing will come up but liquor. He'll sober up. I guess it'll be just three tonight."

"We can't play with him laid out on the table like that," Sloane said.

The three of them hoisted Doogie up by his armpits and dragged him over to the tufted leather sofa. Mr. Elijah put a table-cloth over him. Soon enough, Doogie was feeling no pain. He snoozed like a baby.

"Let's get to it, fellas," Jack announced. "I believe you gentlemen have some of my money in your pockets."

"Ain't you got enough?" Sloane laughed.

"I ain't never got enough. Nothing, and I tell you nothing, is better than the smell of new money, Mr. Governor. Doogie is lucky I don't turn his pockets inside out. I got to make up for that divorce settlement and I'm starting with you," he laughed.

Jack doled out three Dominican cigars and poured another round of whiskey.

"Drink up, boys. It's going to be a bumpy night!"

Elijah dealt the first hand. He had been playing poker a dozen ways since long before the others were more than a twinkle in their mamas' eyes. It was the game of choice for his daddy and uncle in Flat Fork, West Virginia. He'd watched and studied their play in an unpainted lean-to barn with dirt floors lit up by a gas lantern. He was ten before they let him hold a hand of his own.

After two hours of play at a fevered pitch, Sloane was up by a couple of thousand and Elijah was in the hole. Jack, who was holding even, made the mistake of spotting the old geezer a hundred bucks to keep the game going. Elijah rubbed his bald head, turned up his lips and cut the cards. Far too late into the evening, Sloane caught on to Elijah flaring his nostrils whenever he had a winning hand. It seemed almost involuntary. Forty-five minutes later, Elijah had all but cleared the table. Jack threw in his hand first. Sloane took one look at Elijah's widening nostrils and followed suit. He was holding the "nuts."

"Mr. Governor, I think we've just been suckered," Jack said.

"I tell you the truth," Sloane lamented. "I ain't never been whipped like that."

Doogie was starting to wake up.

"Hey, now," he slurred. "When are we going to start the game?"

"Shit!" Sloane laughed.

"And who's been smoking in here?" Doogie asked, fanning the thick fumes with his drunken arms.

"Certainly not you," Jack returned.

Doogie fell off again.

"Probably good for him. Let him sleep it off," Elijah advised. "That woman done broke his heart."

"Shit, just when I was beginning to believe in love," Jack joked.

"In what lifetime?" Sloane shot back. "Hell, I remember when you stuffed five hundred Benjamins into that gal's G-string down at the Pink Pony."

"Now, now, Guv. You've got me all wrong. I'm a believer. I haven't been in a strip club in a hundred years."

"Say it ain't so!" Elijah chimed in.

"In whose church? You just paid your ex-wife fifteen large and you want us to believe you got love on your mind? *'I've got love, love on my mind,'*" Sloane sang off tune, mocking Natalie Cole in a high-pitched voice.

Jack got quiet. Sloane kept singing.

Jack wasn't amused.

"Bruh, I'm just kidding," Sloane said. "We can't predict how the cards will fall."

"Amen to that," Elijah chimed in. "Never can tell."

Sloane got serious. "Listen here, Doc. If Thandy is what you need, then all the money you spent on a divorce was well worth it. *'Ain't no mountain high enough! Ain't no valley low enough,'*" he started singing again.

"I got it bad," Jack admitted.

"It's about time you fessed up to that," said Sloane.

"Did you ever tell her?" Elijah asked.

"I bought her a house and a car, both of which she was only too glad to throw in my face when she left."

"But, did you tell her?" Elijah repeated.

"I guess I didn't," Jack answered.

"Say it with me, Jack. I . . . love . . . you . . . Thandy," Sloane kidded.

Jack smiled.

"It's easy," Sloane said.

"No, it ain't easy," Elijah said. "Not when you're scared."

"I'm not afraid of anything."

"Dr. G, you've been coming to my bar every Friday night for twelve years. Never miss. I've served you enough cognac to drown a city. I've been watching."

"And what did you see?" Jack begged to know.

"I might be wrong, but I ain't too often or too long," Elijah said, sitting up in his high-backed chair. "I remember when you met the girl and didn't even know her phone number. I helped you figure out how to spell her name. I heard it all. I even heard what you didn't say. To tell you the truth, I wondered how long it was going to take you to realize you had something good. I only hoped that it wouldn't be after I was laid out in a funeral parlor and candlelit."

"Have you at least talked to her?" Sloane asked.

"I called once. Sent her roses. She all but told me to take an express bus straight to hell. She's got this big new life. I'm really proud of her. I want her to have everything."

"That's the love I'm talking about!" Elijah beamed.

"You sent flowers? Stop the presses!" Sloane kicked in.

"She doesn't want me," Jack lamented. "She's up there in Chicago. I'm sure some lucky fuck will charm her off her feet. He'll give her what she wants and she'll swoon and scream Hallelujah. I couldn't even take her to the movies."

"I'll bet this whole pile of money that you're wrong about that," Elijah said, pushing his stake to the center of the table. "Picture show or not, I'm willing to bet she's only got eyes for you."

"Sloane?" Jack said, trying to prompt some piece of validation.

"Don't get me into that. She's my friend and I ain't about to break her confidence. But I know she's hurting. That trip to Barbados nearly did her in. But she did say Chicago had its charms."

"The way I see it, you've got one chance, son," Elijah advised. His gruff voice was wise, demanding. "You can make this right now or lose it. That is, if you haven't already."

Jack threw his chips on the table, took a final draw on his cigar, got up abruptly, pushed in his chair, and left.

Chapter 23

The hospital pager pasted to his hip started chirping as he heard his name over the public address system. "Dr. Gabrielle, please report to OR 3!" the charge nurse called into the public address system. "Dr. Jackson Gabrielle, OR 3!"

Jack sprang from the call-room cot and sprinted down the wide corridor quicker than Michael Vick could wiggle his way out of an intercepted pass. He made it to the operating room just as the patient began seizing. The body bucked and convulsed. A nurse pumped medication through the IV and he steadied. Another attendant quickly scrubbed his already bald head with antiseptic foam as Sandy rushed in.

Jack read through the brief medical chart, then went right to work. He carefully cut back the scalp as a surgical nurse set up a high-powered microscope. Once inside, Jack was unnerved. The already thin walls of the intracranial aneurysm were on the verge of rupture. His hands began to twitch. Sandy stood next to him. Her presence steadied him. The bleeding and water flooded the brain, but the sack of arterial blood, though dangerously thin, was thankfully still intact. Using the three-dimensional mapping on the overhead monitor, he cautiously moved through the tissue until the monster was fully revealed, a tiny balloon of blood in the frontal lobe. His hands froze.

"Is everything all right, Dr. Gabrielle?" a resident physician asked.

"Absolutely. Let's get to it," Jack said, blowing out a deep gust.

Sandy stepped away to turn on the stereo and slipped a CD into the spinner.

"Buddy you're a boy make a big noise . . . !"

Satisfied with the volume, Jack went back to work. He examined and placed a small metallic clip across the base of the balloon. Once the neck of the bubble was secured, he took another deep breath and began to reconstruct the artery wall to maintain blood flow to the brain. The remaining blood and fluid were suctioned away. Sandy watched Jack.

"You got mud on yo face! You big disgrace! Somebody better put you back in your place!"

Close to an hour later, Jack began closing the tissue. He replaced the skull and secured it with titanium screws, then set about stitching the scalp. He was sweating. His scrub shirt was drenched like he'd taken a swim in the English Channel. He felt his legs wobble.

"Good job, everyone," he said, locking his knees.

The team began to exit the room.

"Why does he need music?" a young resident physician asked.

"It helps him concentrate," Sandy threw out.

"Go figure," the young doctor returned. "I couldn't focus. I got worried there for a moment."

"You should never worry about Dr. Gabrielle," Sandy assured.

Jack went immediately to the private waiting room, where he met Mrs. Rosen, the patient's wife, who was by then joined by five of her eight children. The others were en route.

"I'm Dr. Gabrielle," he said, extending his hand to shake hers.

The Rosen family stood up. Gerrie Rosen threw her arms

around him, but said nothing. He had expected and prepared for tears. There were none.

Bertie Rosen's oldest son, Bert Jr., peppered questions. Jack sat down in a waiting-room chair and began to answer. He was surrounded by Rosen children.

"We don't understand medical mumbo jumbo," Sarah, the middle girl, said. "We need it straight. Daddy taught us to shoot straight."

"Your father got here just in time," Jack said. "We were able to prevent rupture. He'll need several weeks of therapy."

"And then what?" Sarah begged to know.

"And then he'll need to take it easy. He doesn't smoke, does he?"

"Not since last summer," Mrs. Rosen chimed in.

"Don't let him start again," Jack advised. "No heavy exercise. I will assign him to an ICU bed for a few days, then move him to a standard room."

"I've had him for forty years and I'll have forty more, God willing," Gerrie sighed. "I don't know what life is without him and I don't want to know."

Gerrie Rosen had never driven a clutch in her life. Bertie had always done the driving. They married two days before he shipped out for Marine Corps boot camp, vowing never to spend another day apart. After twenty years in the service, he retired and took a job cutting timber for Georgia Pacific. Every day for forty years and counting, her husband had seen to her every need, even in the early years when love was all they had for dinner. Together they had raised eight children, sent them all to college, watched them get married, and delighted in their grandbabies. If they were lucky, Gerrie thought, they would be around to see the great-grands. Albert got a retirement package from Georgia Pacific when the company was sold to a global conglomerate. The two of them spent their days tending to their treasured vegetable gardens and traveled when they could. Destin, Florida, was Gerrie's favorite place on earth. Just the day before, she'd finally gotten her husband to say yes to a time-share on the beach.

He didn't like all that mess he'd heard about hurricanes, but he'd do anything for his Gerrie. That night, she'd made him a nice dinner of his favorite pot roast and roasted potatoes, watched *Wheel of Fortune* and *Let's Make a Deal* reruns and gone off to bed unaware of the time bomb ticking in his head. She was too tired to stay up to watch *American Idol* with him.

She heard him call her name just after midnight. It sounded like a whisper at first and she thought she was dreaming. When he called again, this time painfully stronger, she leapt up from their bed and went out to the living room where she found him slumped over the coffee table clutching his head.

Gerrie loaded him into the Ford F-150. Bertie shuddered in the passenger seat and began to convulse and vomit. Gerrie was frightened. The truck jerked and stalled a few times before she got a handle on the gears. She fumbled her way straight to Northside Hospital.

Jack joined the Rosen family for the second time in the same waiting room. The stent had given way. Blood poured into the brain. Bert Rosen died before the team could get him back into surgery.

"I'm sorry for your loss, Mrs. Rosen," Jack offered.

"No, Dr. Gabrielle. We're celebrating his life. What a blessing it was to have him with us."

The family formed a circle and prayed. Jack joined them.

Chapter 24

"Doubt thou the stars are fire; doubt that the sun doth move; doubt truth to be a liar; but never doubt I love."

Thandy was stunned to find Jack standing on her doorstep, bundled up to his earlobes in a shepherd's coat, shivering like a washing machine on final spin, and quoting Shakespeare. The snow fell from the gray sky in buckets as Thandy stood gaping at Jack in disbelief.

"Is that any way to treat a man who trekked through a blizzard to get here?"

"You're pathetic. You know that, don't you?"

"That I am," he conceded.

The wind chill made it feel like a hundred below; the cars on the street were covered in blankets of white. Thandy hadn't been outside in a few days. The entire city was paralyzed. Mayor Daley had issued a curfew until city workers could clear and salt the pavement. Montana was stuck at a girlfriend's house, unable to drive home in the snow.

Thandy wondered how Jack had made it to Chicago. He wriggled his fingers in the duty-free shop gloves he'd picked up to make sure he could still move them.

"Uh, come in. It's cold out there."

Thandy opened the door a little wider and waved him inside. The house was warm with fireplace-cooked air. The aroma of freshly baked bread emanated from the kitchen. Music streamed from the surround sound system and filled every room. Jack followed her through the comfortably furnished living room and into the kitchen. She went about the business of brewing another pot of coffee while he sat on a bar stool under a carousel of clay pots that hung from the ceiling, admiring the elegant home. A half read novel lay facedown on the countertop. At first, they said nothing. She caught, then tried to ignore, his stares.

"Your house is beautiful."

"Thank you."

After a few minutes of waiting for the earth to move, he asked, "Where's Montana?"

She didn't answer. She swallowed and filled the brewer with water. He admired her slimmed figure.

"So, are you going to tell me how you got here in five feet of snow when every airport north of Memphis is closed?"

"Lucky, I guess. I got the last flight out yesterday, before it got jammed up. I got in after midnight and stayed at the O'Hare Marriott. We couldn't get into Midway."

"And how did you get here? I'm a long way from O'Hare."

"Snowplow."

She turned to him. "What do you mean a snowplow?"

"I paid a guy and he went for his cousin. The guy works for the city."

"And what if I wasn't at home?"

"It's a snowstorm. Everybody's at home."

She smiled at the stove.

"I'm sorry," he said to her back. He took off his coat and gloves.

"You've already said that," she returned, leaning over the counter, studying the pot of coffee.

"I meant it," he said, undoing the wool scarf to let his earlobes warm.

"Thanks. That really clears things up."

Jack grew silent. He never needed anyone before. And if he did, he had never admitted it.

"Why did you come here?"

"I thought . . ." he started.

She finished it for him. "You thought you could just get on a plane, bribe your way to my house, and then waltz in here, quote some dead ass poet, and I would just melt. Right?"

"No."

"Of course, you did." She turned around and faced him. "Admit it. I'm just the fish that got away. You've never had to want for anything, Jack Gabrielle," she said, waving her newly sculpted arms around. "Not for food, not for the light bill. You haven't gone a single day without everything you needed, everything you could have wanted. You need a ride in the snow. Money no object. That's worth one to five, hard time. But if you get caught, you won't go to jail. The poor schmuck who took your money will. You'll just buy your way out. You've never had to struggle for anything."

"And you have?" he dismissed. "I read the article. Hell, Thandy, you make as much money as I do, even more. Oh, I forgot. This is your kingdom. Nothing happens that you don't control."

"I earn it, every day."

"Of course, you do. If they knew what they were really getting, they'd double your salary."

"You don't know the half!" she exploded. "You spend so much time worrying about what you want that you can't see anybody else."

"That isn't true."

"Of course it is! You don't know what I had to do to get here!" she yelled. "You never had anybody ask you to fuck him in exchange for fixing a hot water heater so your baby could have a warm bath. And look at this," she cried, yanking her hair back from her temple. "Look at it! Damn it! Look at it!" Her scar stood out despite years of fade creams.

He wanted to touch her, but knew better.

"Thandy, I'm sorry," he said, pouring more liquid over his vowels.

"You keep saying that, but you don't even know what to be sorry for. My father did this to me. He beat me until I bled. And then he kept on. My mama watched. I was pregnant with Montana then. At fucking fifteen, I moved to Atlanta and got married to the only man who never wanted anything from me. By the time I was nineteen, he was in jail doing life times three. I was broke and homeless, living at some stay-n-play motel, fighting to get my baby back!"

"I can't change what happened to you."

"I never thought you could."

"I need you," he said.

She swallowed hard.

"This isn't about you. It's about me, Jack. For the first time in my life, it's all about me. It's about my life and my child—everything that belongs to me. This is about my house, the one I bought with my money. It's about my *everything*. This scar is mine, too. It's about everything nobody can take from me. It ain't about what you can give me. It's about what I can give myself. It's about my dignity."

"Running won't save your dignity."

"Fuck you!"

He searched her face. He'd never looked at it before, but the scar seemed larger. The smooth brown trail of tissue running across her right temple was slightly darker than the rest of her face.

Thandy shook her head and went for the coffee. She poured two cups and took the overly browned loaf of bread out of the oven. They sat across the kitchen island from each other, pulling away warm chunks. Alternately they stared into the empty mugs and at one another. There was silence for the next hour.

"Sloane told me what happened," Jack said first.

"It's over now and I'm fine."

He got up and warmed more coffee.

She waved her hand. "I don't want anymore," she said.

Jack sat down and let his cup go cold. He was thinking about Angel's bag of tricks and how she tried to finagle her way into the good life. He wondered how long Thandy knew she was pregnant, but couldn't bring himself to ask.

"Sloane shouldn't have said anything."

"He's your friend. He was just trying to help."

"The road to hell is paved with good intentions," she said with a wry smile.

"I wish I could've been here. You know I love you."

"I know no such thing! You love *you*, Jack Gabrielle."

"C'mon, Thandy. You don't mean that."

"Just leave. Call your snowplow buddies and get out."

"Is that what you want? You didn't give me the choice to be here," he said.

"The hell I didn't! Nobody forced you to get on a plane to Barbados! What was I supposed to do? Suck it up? Forget about it? You made your choice when you got on that plane."

Thandy looked up and into his eyes. She didn't know the Jack she saw.

"I don't want to fight," he said.

Her tears were rising when she got up from the island. "I don't blame you."

"You have every right to."

"But I don't. I don't have that kind of energy. I don't have any fight left. I put it all out there on that running trail."

"Maybe you should let yourself get mad at something."

"How would you know what I need?" she said, looking him square in the eyes. "Just how long are you going to be in Chicago?"

"Until you can honestly tell me that you don't love me," he answered.

Her eyes flooded. She smeared away the snot and tears with her hands. "I don't. Now go."

"I don't believe you."

"Please go."

Jack didn't move.

"Listen, I don't know when Montana will make it home," she whispered. "The ice is pretty bad out there. You shouldn't be here when she gets home and I need to pull myself together."

"After all this time, you still haven't told her about us?"

"What was I supposed to say? Was I supposed to tell her that I didn't think enough of myself to find a man who loved me? One that didn't have a wife at home?"

"You're going to throw me out in the snow?" he grinned. "It's a cold, cruel world out there."

"Tell me about it."

"Look at me and tell me you don't love me."

The next several hours were endless. Against her better judgment, she allowed Jack to stay. But there was no way to explain it to Philly, no way to explain it even to herself. But there they lay on the sectional sofa, entangled in each other, when Montana came home. She took one look at her mother and the stranger and went upstairs to her room. She knew immediately that the man downstairs was the mysterious Jack.

Jack slowly untangled himself, got up, and followed Montana to her room.

"Hi, Montana," he said. "I'm Jack Gabrielle."

"I know who you are," she said dryly.

"You do, do you?"

He eased in her doorway.

"I'm seventeen, not stupid."

"Can I come in?"

"I don't care what you do."

She was just as tough as her mother. Jack took a seat on the edge of the bed. Montana plopped down on a pile of stuffed bears.

"I remember you, you know. You drove us to North Carolina when my grandpa died. I was twelve."

"Yes, I did. You have a good memory."

"I remember what you told her," she said, folding her arms around a stuffed kitten. "You told her you would take care of us. That you wouldn't let any harm come her way. You were talking about getting married and having babies."

"I remember."

"Coming here will only make it worse when you leave. She doesn't need this."

"I'm trying to get it right."

"She lost the baby, you know?"

"I know."

"I don't even think she knew she was pregnant. She started running when we got here. Every night after dinner."

"Promise me something?"

"Like what?"

"Never give her a reason to worry about you."

Jack left the room, tipped back down the stairs, and returned to the sofa. Thandy was still fast asleep. He pushed back her hair and kissed her forehead. When he kissed the scar, she jerked and woke up.

"Go home, Jack," she muttered still half asleep. "Go home."

"Shhhh," he said, kissing her face again.

Thandy settled in and fell back to sleep. Jack remained awake, watching her as she slept. He ran his finger along the scar. For the first time, he realized that perfection lies in the imperfections. After a few hours, he lifted her and took her upstairs. He undressed her and laid her in the bed. He crawled in beside her. They slept until dawn. They made love when the sun came up.

"Good morning," he smiled.

She snuggled under his shoulder, taking in his scent. The snowblowers were going outside the window. Neighborhood children were giggling and tossing snowballs. She had no compulsion to go outside. No urge to get out of bed. It was Sunday morning, a week before Christmas, and there was nothing on the day's agenda. Jack pulled the covers over their naked bodies and tugged her in closer, gripping his fingers around hers. With her head under his, she stared at their clenched hands. Montana could be heard padding about down the hall.

"I don't know what to tell her," Thandy whispered.

"I don't think you have to say anything."

"Yeah, I do. I have to tell her who you are."

"She already knows. I talked to her last night."

She jolted with panic.

"It's okay, I promise," he assured. "She already knew who I was. You'd be surprised. I guess I've got some work to do."

They stayed under the covers well beyond noon. Thandy squirmed around, half wanting to stay in bed, half wanting to get up and run. She let out a soft moan.

"Tell me what hurts, baby," he said.

She looked up at him. His eyes were closed. He was waiting for an answer, something not already said. The truth was everything hurt, but the worst was over, she assured herself. Thandy climbed out of bed and went into the bathroom. He followed.

She wasn't willing to admit that she was tired. She was tired of a career, tired of hundred-hour weeks, tired of trying to prove to the world that she could take anything. She didn't want to admit that she simply wanted a husband, that she wanted Montana to have a father who would be there all of the time. She couldn't admit that she still loved Jack, more than she wanted to, more than she loved even herself sometimes. Still there remained a residue of disappointment that never completely drained away.

Thandy remembered the people who helped her float, encouraged her to swim—Phillipa and Sloane. They were the people who had been there when she couldn't be there for herself. They were the ones that reminded her of her own beauty, that told her nothing was impossible. They were faithful believers when she thought she had nothing left. Even when she felt like she was blowing away, they were there like anchors in a hurricane.

And then there was Jack. He didn't even know the wind was blowing hard. Afraid he would cut and run, she had refused to let him see the imperfections, she'd hidden all the scars. The pain of the miscarriage had gone. Now Jack was here and so was the ache. She hadn't really wanted a baby. Montana had been and still was enough. But even after she got a clean bill of health, her heart was still mourning the loss.

He walked up behind her, placed his hands on her hands around her belly, and said, "I never knew what I wanted. But the day I saw you, I knew it was you. It had always been you."

They watched each other, together, in the mirror. No high-powered jobs, no fancy homes, no swanky cars. Just naked.

She closed her eyes, shook her head, and said, "What do you want from me?"

He thought for a moment, then said, "I want you to come home."

He turned her around, put his arms around her body and wept against her. She had never heard him cry before. It felt like she was locked in the arms of a perfect stranger.

They spent the holidays together. Thandy got her first Christmas morning with Jack. And they were inseparable through the new year. On New Year's Day, after he caught her looking at him one too many times during breakfast, he asked, "What's on your mind?"

"I just wanted to make sure you were still here."

"I love you," he said finally. "I don't want to wake up another morning without you."

Chapter 25

Yvetta was working the lid of a mason jar when the call came. The vinegar stewed tomatoes, pot roast, and stone-ground grits she was making for Fields would have to wait. Cump was dead. He went to sleep, still dressed in his overalls, watching the evening news and never woke up.

"Oh, Daddy," she whispered as she hung up the phone.

Yvetta took off her apron and placed the unopened jar on the windowsill over the sink. She shuffled into her bedroom and searched the closets for the tan suit she knew he would want to be buried in. She found it and pressed it out, running the steam iron along the seams until the slacks could stand up by themselves. Cump would have wanted it that way. She spent hours on the phone, poring through her address book, calling one relative after another. She called the number she had for Thandy in Chicago and was surprised when a man answered.

"I believe I must have the wrong number."

"Mrs. Malone?"

"Jackson?"

"Yes ma'am. Thandy isn't here right now, but I can tell her you called."

"Thank you," she said. "Tell her it's very important, would you?"

"Yes ma'am."

"Her grandfather passed on last night."

"I'm so sorry."

"He's in a better place now, Jackson."

A short time later, the house was brimming with people, everybody she knew and some she didn't. Grace held down the kitchen as various mourners brought food and a good word. Yvetta didn't care for any of it, really. The sooner they were all gone, the better. She paced the kitchen and waited for the phone to ring.

A light blanket of snow was falling as if God was shaking cake flour through a metal sifter when they walked in. Yvonne was unbundling her daughters and pulling their little feet out of their yellow rubber boots.

"Sissy!"

"Hello, Yvonne," Thandy said, looking away.

"Sweet Jesus," Yvetta muttered when she heard her daughters' voices. "Thank you, Lord Jesus, thank you."

Yvetta sat down at the dining room table and stared at the lace doilies. Thandy walked up behind her and wrapped her arms around her mother's shoulders.

"It's good to have you home."

"I've been gone too long."

"Jackson, it's good to see you, too," Yvetta said politely. "Where's my granddaughter?"

Montana stepped inside the front door.

"Lord, have mercy," Yvetta said, wrapping her arms around Montana, who hugged her back as if she'd known her all of her life.

"Girl, give your big sister a hug," Yvonne interrupted.

The women embraced long enough to feel like sisters again.

"I hear you got a fancy new job up in Chicago. You're doing

big things. Never would have known it the way you were catting around here."

"That's enough, Vonnie," her mother said.

Thandy wanted to tell her sister that it was just a job and that she knew Vonnie had done some catting of her own; their parents just didn't know about it.

"And Montana is so big! Girl, you look just like your father. I'm your aunt Vonnie. You weren't even born when . . ."

"I said that's enough, Yvonne," her mother said again.

Montana took off her coat and sat on the sofa. Grace saw after the guests and offered Montana something to drink. She declined politely.

Jack faded off into the kitchen and made small talk with Fields.

"How long y'all plan to be around here?" the older man asked.

"Just until after the memorial service," Jack returned. "We're heading back to Atlanta in the morning."

"I always knew she had another daughter. Haven't had the pleasure of meeting her."

"It's been a long time."

"I'd say that's the honest to God's truth. What do you do down there in Atlanta?"

"I'm a surgeon, sir."

"Is that right?"

"Yes, sir."

"Then you know how to mend a broken heart."

"I'm working on it," Jack said.

After evening supper, most of the family took to the living room. As more people poured through the front door and into the small space, Montana put her coat back on and went outside. Jack followed.

"You know my mother better than anybody," she said, walking toward the gate.

"I'd like to think so. But I think I run a distant second to you."

"My mother is an expert in compartmentalizing things. She doesn't even like it when her food runs together," she joked. "It's cold out here. You should get your coat."

"I guess we've all got our secrets," he shivered.

"Did she ever tell you anything about my father?"

"No. No, she didn't. You never met him?"

"I don't even know his name," Montana said, leaning over the metal gatepost. "I figure he must be around here somewhere or at least he used to be."

"I'm sure she's got her reasons."

Thandy stepped out onto the porch and said, "None of them are good enough."

"Mom, I . . ." Montana said, embarrassment rising in her cheeks.

"It's all right, baby."

Jack tipped his head and went back inside.

"I don't know where to start," Thandy said, advancing down the walkway.

"I just want to know, Mama."

"Well, for starters his name is your name: Montana. He used to live a few blocks from here. His father owned a car wash in the middle of town. Miss Grace said they tore it down last fall and built a new Walgreens."

"Did you love him?"

"With everything I had. And he loved me. You are the apple of his eye."

"Then why isn't he here?"

"He can't be here, honey," Thandy said. "I'm sure he would be if he could. But he can't."

"He isn't dead too, is he?"

"No, honey." She took a deep breath. "Your father is in prison," Thandy admitted. "He's been in jail since you were almost three years old."

After a moment of silence, Montana spoke in a whisper. "What did he do?"

"I'd like to tell you, but maybe he should."

"He didn't kill anybody, did he?"

"No. He's not that kind of man."

"What is he like?"

"He's beautiful. Just like you. Everything about him is just beautiful. He was so cute, he could stop traffic. We got married when I was almost sixteen. I was already pregnant." Thandy wondered how she could recite a lifetime on a wintery porch.

"Are you going to marry Dr. Jack?"

"I can't say, honey. I do know that there have been days when all I ever wanted was to be married."

"Why didn't you?"

"The stars never lined up right. It's complicated. But, I owe you some answers. When this is all over, I promise we'll talk and keep talking until you have all of your answers."

They went back inside. Thandy motioned her mother into the bedroom. Montana trailed behind her.

"What is it, baby?" Yvetta said as she clicked on the light.

"Montana needs to see the box."

"What box?"

"You know what box I'm talking about," Thandy said, tossing up a suspicious eyebrow.

Yvetta went into her closet and dug under a pile of blankets. She pulled the box from the closet and placed it on the bed.

"This stuff has been in there for ages," Yvetta said. "I guess it's time for us to take a look. Funny thing is I never could find it before. The Lord works in mysterious ways."

"Indeed," Thandy whispered.

Yvetta opened the cardboard flaps and pulled out a pile of letters. Thandy's law school graduation invitation was one of the unopened envelopes. There were pictures of Simon when he was a boy and others of the girls going to church on Easter Sunday. There were several pictures of Montana when she was a baby, all clearly marked with her age and weight.

"I don't care what nobody says. This baby looks just like you, Thandy. If them ain't Cump's eyes . . ."

She kept digging until she found a large brown envelope. She handed it to Thandy, who opened it. Inside was a stack of photos. Some were of Thandy by herself and others with Monty.

"That's him," Thandy said.

Montana stared at the Polaroid a long time. Yvetta and Thandy looked at her, waiting for something.

"Can I keep it?"

"Sure you can," her grandmother said. "You can take anything you want."

"I just want this picture and that one," she said, pointing to a picture of Yvetta and Thandy.

"You can have them, baby," Yvetta said.

"Mom, can we go see him?"

"I don't know," Thandy replied. She got up from the bed.

"Why not?"

"Your father never wanted you to see him in prison. He made me promise."

Yvetta lowered her eyebrows and said, "Take that child right on up there to see her father."

Yvetta gave Thandy a stern but loving look.

"I'll call and get clearance. We'll have to put our names on the list and your father will have to say it is okay. He can be very stubborn."

"Ain't that the truth," Yvetta said.

"Mama, what's that supposed to mean?"

"I tried to run that boy away from here," Yvetta smiled. "But he wouldn't go. He was just as stubborn as my Simon."

Thandy had never heard her mother compare Monty—or anyone—to Simon. She couldn't believe her ears. "And I'll tell you something else," Yvetta continued. "That man out there loves you."

Montana chimed in. "Grandma, he came all the way to Chicago in a snowstorm. Mama was gonna kick him out on his ass. I mean, his behind."

"Honey, are you going back to Atlanta with Jackson? Isn't he . . . ?

"No, Mama, he isn't."

"You're not going to give up your job, are you?"

"After the funeral, we're going home. I'll commute for a while and see how things work out."

"You know, I ain't nothing about all that flying."

Two days later, the Malone family gathered in silence around the casket. Henry Tecumseh Cole was laid to rest in the churchyard, next to his precious Myrtle and his older brother Harry. The breeze rustled the treetops and loosened the soft thin sheet of snow from the limbs. Townsfolk and other relations came over the hill, their shoes snapping the icy white grass. A line of black limos glistened in the winter sun. The funeral home director readied the stands of floral arrangements with large pastel ribbons and placed them around the casket.

Yvonne and her husband rode in the second funeral car. Grace and Fields came together in her Cadillac. All of Cump's surviving children and their children made the trip from as far away as California. But mostly Yvetta felt alone. She had been his sole caregiver for more years than she wanted to remember. He hadn't been in any pain, the nursing home administrator told her. And she was glad for it.

His sight had diminished to mere shadows over recent days. But in his mind's eye lay a perfect vision of the granddaughter he cajoled with butterscotch candies. He never forgot Thandy's playful smile, her mischievous nature, and how much she loved the snow.

Each January, Cump would gather some fresh snow from the yard, make a large round ball, and store it in the deep freezer. By March, when winter was gone, Thandy would wait next to the large white box while he dug inside for the foil-wrapped ball of ice. Every year, he saved a bit of January for her. She was his January girl.

The snow was coming down hard now, so thick, Yvetta could barely see her cousin Caledonia, who had come all the way from

Texas to be there. The white roses and lilies were beautiful, Yvetta thought. As the pastor started the eulogy, Thandy took her mother's hand and squeezed it. Yvetta tilted her head and laid it on her shoulder. For the first time since the call came from Shady Oaks, Yvetta wept. When the service ended, the two women walked to the first funeral car, escorted by the preacher. Montana walked a few paces behind. Jack was holding her hand. The stream of cars made its way through the streets and onto Delmar.

"You've been in jail? You're kidding, right?"

"I swear to God," Thandy said, crossing her heart. "Hope to die."

He opened his arms and she kicked off her shoes and got into bed with him. They were still dressed in their funeral clothes. Jack listened intently as Thandy told her story.

"I've got my very own, personal superhero."

"Who knew?" she laughed.

"You chased him out of the house with a knife?"

"Sure did. He should have shut up and fixed my pipes."

Jack stretched his body across the hotel bed. "I'll fix your pipes."

Thandy pulled herself closer and lay on his chest.

"You actually snuck back into that house to look for that money?"

"Of course I did."

"You say that like people violate crime scenes every day."

"My house was not a crime scene."

"The marshals had it padlocked, didn't they?"

"Yup."

"And it had been seized by the court, right?"

"Yup."

"So you just broke in?"

"Yup."

"Who taught you how to pick a lock?"

"My grandfather."

"Jesus Christ. And then, let me get this straight, you gave all the money to your husband's lawyer."

"It was his money."

"You are the most honest cat burglar I know."

"I'm the only cat burglar you know."

She could hear their laughs echo in his chest.

"You're right about that." He closed his eyes and asked, "Do you remember the day we met?"

"You mean the day you started stalking me?"

"I resent that. I am not a stalker."

"I don't remember inviting you to Chicago. I never told you where I lived."

"A man has his sources. That's my story and I'm sticking to it."

"I owe Sloane a good ass kicking."

"You can't just go punch the governor of Georgia."

"Watch me!"

They laughed until they couldn't breathe. Jack thought his chest was going to explode.

"Are you sure this is what you really want?" she asked, collecting her wind. "You want to spend the rest of your life with a convict?"

"Absolutely, jail bird," he chuckled. "Just don't make me stay in another Motel 6."

Chapter 26

The Honorable Judge P. Maulpin Arrington entered the crowded courtroom. He took his place at the head of his kingdom. He scanned the docket and ordered the bailiff to call the first case. The Gabrielles and their hired guns stepped forward. Etienne stood with Finlayson on the left, Jack with Parham on the right. Etienne and Jack examined one another from five feet, the closest they had been in months. He was surprised at her zeal. He hadn't expected her fight.

Even though the proceedings were just a formality, Jack was sweating under his fine tailored suit. Not too cheap, not too overwhelming—just as Parham had prescribed. Etienne, on the other hand, was dressed in a four-button, cobalt blue St. John and black slingback heels. He couldn't help but stare. She was the woman he had once pledged his life to, forsaking all others. Now she just wanted to give him a good ass whipping that even money couldn't buy. Five minutes in, Jack checked his watch. The judge was taking his time. The filing was straightforward. No claim that the soon-to-be-former Mrs. Gabrielle would have to fend for herself in a soup kitchen.

The judge kept nodding and saying "uhn uhn" to himself.

His glasses slid down to the tip of his nose. Jack grew anxious. Etienne was stoic. At one point the day before, while sitting in Parham's office as he directed him to change the beneficiaries on his life insurance policies and make Thandy the sole heir to his estate, Jack stumbled on a bit of remorse. He regretted his part in Etienne's pain. He understood she started drinking in some part due to him. She hadn't had a drink in months, Finlayson assured him before he agreed to joint custody.

"Mrs. Gabrielle, Dr. Gabrielle," the judge started.

"Yes, your honor," they said in unison.

"I understand you have come to mutually agreeable financial terms."

"Yes, your honor."

"And with respect to your sons, Jackson and Jacob, you have agreed to joint custody?"

"Yes, your honor," the attorneys said.

"So noted."

There was a gap of silence.

"It never pleases me to grant a petition for divorce. But that's my job. I have reviewed this case and find that there are no legal barriers to granting your request."

The attorneys nodded.

"It grieves me when there are children involved."

Arrington looked down at the paperwork and up again at the petitioners.

"So granted," he said, banging the gavel.

Jack shook Parham's hand and left the courtroom. Thandy was waiting in the vestibule. Jack grabbed her up by the waist and spun her around until she was dizzy.

"Baby, it's over," he said.

Etienne came out of the courtroom just in time to witness their jubilation. Jack's head was still spinning from the impromptu twirl and he was wild-eyed and stumbling like a drunk. She wanted to put her hands around his throat. Finlayson led her away.

Jack and Thandy left the courthouse together.

ॶ ॶ ॶ

The house was even more than Thandy had imagined, more beautiful than any she had ever seen. The interior was an eclectic mix of styles, including Italian Renaissance, French Rococo, and contemporary African American. A woman's hand was evident in the selection of draperies and various works of art that adorned the walls. A grand, wood-carved stairway erupted from the marble-lined foyer and curved to its zenith, opening to an overly wide hallway laden with priceless artworks. The stucco and stacked stone house had at least eight bedrooms. The carriage house boasted two more. The two-story master suite had a private Jacuzzi tub with cedar trim, a book-lined study and an entry to the balcony. Outside, the lawn stretched from the curbside like an ocean of green. There were four buildings in all and Thandy was certain it would take months before she saw it all. The house staff, led by Senora Perez, busied themselves readying the house for their arrival.

A second master bedroom was given to Montana. Jack filled it with all of her favorite things. He left a copy of the Physician's Desk Reference on her nightstand and framed the photos her grandmother had given her.

All eight fireplaces were ablaze; new linens were placed on every bed; there were fresh vases of flowers in every room. It was January, but it felt more like springtime. The smells of jasmine and vanilla filled the house.

"It's beautiful," Thandy said. "It's just beautiful."

"My father built it fifty years ago. I've lived here every day of my life. Mother gave it to me as a wedding gift."

Thandy watched from an upper window as a driver continued unloading their bags from the car. She then went about hanging her clothes on the empty side of the expansive, custom-built closet.

"We don't have to stay here," Jack offered as she hung her dresses. "We can buy another house. Just tell me what you want."

"No," she demurred. "The boys need some level of consistency. When will they get here?"

"I'll pick them up later this afternoon. I'm sure it will be love at first sight."

Thandy looked into his eyes. "I love everything you ever gave breath to."

"And I love you for it."

Senora Perez spent the better part of the afternoon preparing paella, Jack's favorite, while he went for the boys. Thandy lent her a hand. Together, the women diced vegetables, shelled shrimp, and cleaned mussels, while Montana sipped cocoa in the keeping room.

"Mom, are you going to cook all the time?"

"As often as you want me to."

"Are you going to quit your job?"

"I don't know yet."

"What are you going to do? Be some kind of virtual, jet-setting CEO?" Montana joked.

"Something like that," Thandy smiled. "For a while anyway."

"How many children does Dr. Jack have?"

"Two sons, Jackson and Jacob," she answered. "Jack is twelve and Jacob will be six next month. And before you ask, I've never met them."

Just after seven o'clock, the soon-to-be Gabrielle family sat for dinner. A bit sheepish at first, the boys could barely say their names. That changed when Senora Perez led them to the table of food. To their father's delight, little Jack and Jacob quickly stuffed their mouths with yellow rice and sausage. Montana barely touched her food. Jack was concerned.

"What's wrong, honey?" Thandy asked.

"When are we going?" Montana muttered.

"Going where?" Jack asked.

"To see my father. You promised."

"Well, I don't know," Thandy answered.

"We can go next week," Jack said.

"But you're on call," Thandy said. "You've been out of the office almost a month."

"And a few more days won't hurt. Did you get the clearance? Maybe Sloane can give us a hand."

"I'm sure he would," Thandy said. "It's okay to go back to work."

"Daddy, what's clearance?" little Jack asked.

Jack couldn't think of an answer right away.

"It's like the permission slip they give you at school when you go on a field trip," Thandy answered.

"Miss Thandy, are you going to take us on a field trip?" Jacob asked.

"No, son," Jack answered.

"We wanna go!" little Jack chirped.

"But this trip is for the big people," Thandy said.

"How come only big people get to go?" little Jack pressed.

"Just this time. Next time, you can go. And you'll get to pick where we go."

"Can we go to Disney World?" asked Jacob.

"We'll see. But only if you are good boys," Thandy said.

"We'll be good!" the boys exclaimed in unison.

Jack smiled. He was taken with the way Thandy answered their questions.

"Do we have to call you Mommy?" Jackson asked.

"Not if you don't want to," Thandy answered. "You still have a mommy who loves you very much."

"I want to!" Jacob chirped. "You're nice!"

The family continued eating. Jack could only watch and admire Thandy as she ate.

"Senora Perez? Are you available to watch the boys tomorrow evening?" Jack asked.

"Sí, Doctor Gabrielle. Senora Gabrielle, is there something special you would like me to prepare for breakfast?"

"No, no. Don't trouble yourself," Thandy answered. "I'll see after breakfast."

"Where are you going, Mom?"

"I don't know. Jack?" she asked. "Where are we going?"

"The Atlanta Medical Association Ball."

The idea caught her off-guard. She'd never been allowed to go to public events with Jack. She was so accustomed to ducking and hiding in the shadows that she didn't know what to say. And now she and Montana were living in his house. And the maid was calling her *Senora* Gabrielle. And little Jacob wanted to call her Mommy. She loved the very sound of it. Jack hadn't proposed, but for the first time she really wanted him to. She wanted to walk into the ballroom with her head held high and sit next to him on the dais. She hadn't even allowed herself to imagine it before.

"I don't have anything to wear."

"Yes, you do. I hope you don't mind, but I picked up something this morning."

"How do you know what size I wear?"

"I know everything about you."

The boys giggled.

"Of course, Sloane and his wife are coming. We're presenting him with a special honor."

"You're just full of surprises, aren't you?"

When dinner was through, Thandy and Senora Perez took the boys for a bath. Thandy read them a story and after another round of questions about the field trip, they drifted off to sleep. Jack stood in the doorway listening.

"Thank you, baby," Jack whispered.

"For what?"

"For loving them," he said. "And me. I know that I . . ."

"Shhhh," she said, placing her fingers to his lips. "It's over now. We're home."

Peering over his shoulder, she saw it.

"Jack! You didn't." A flowing silk Versace gown hung from the bed's canopy frame.

"Try it on, baby."

"But Jack, it's too much."

"When you're in love, it's never too much."

Jack kissed her into the master suite. He kissed her kneecaps first then worked his way up until she wet up the sheets with a hallelujah chorus. They made love for hours on end as their children slept down the long hallway. Satisfied that all was as it should be, they drifted off to sleep, too.

Chapter 27

Angel slid into a pair of snug-fit, lowrider Seven jeans. She faced the full-length mirror, half admiring the way the material embraced her curves, and half admiring that the jeans would not be Jack's preference. He hated denim. She wrapped her very perfect breasts in a silk backless halter that revealed the cuts and curves she'd spent hours in the gym honing to perfection. Her skin was wonderfully bronzed and glowing thanks to several sun-soaked hours lying nearly naked next to the lake. The incredible sight caught the attention of hotel guests—at least the men.

"There is a God," one said as he sipped a Long Island Iced Tea on the veranda.

As she left the hotel room, Angel dropped her cell phone on the nightstand just in case he called. She didn't want to be around if it rang. She didn't want to care if it didn't. He hadn't called in weeks. Jack never once returned her messages.

She headed down to the lobby bar for a nightcap. She needed a perfect stranger to look at her and say she had wonderful eyes. By now, the bar was full of conference attendees and Angel was too good to miss. The getaway to Lake Oconee had been Stephanie's idea.

"All you need is money for the hotel room," Stephanie advised. "Let the rest happen. The hotel will be full of perfectly willing brothas—at least a hundred of them."

Thanks to the annual 100 Black Men of Atlanta retreat, Stephanie was absolutely correct in her assumption. No wives or girlfriends would be present and thus Angel would have her pickings.

"You gotta get your numbers up," Stephanie counseled. "Get back in the game."

Angel had been to the Ritz-Carlton at Reynolds Plantation only once before—with Jack. She was glad to be spending the night in a familiar hotel. It wasn't the first time she'd left Atlanta in search of greener pastures. More than once, she'd jetted off to one conference or another in search of Mr. Right. But when it was over, she always felt empty. She'd convinced herself that Jack was Mr. Right. He didn't have to give her everything, just enough. Jack came and went when he pleased. He gave her little and made it seem like the world.

All she wanted now was to forget it ever happened.

After she got out of jail, she tried calling him. When he didn't answer, she cried for days. Months of sneaking off to the beach and stolen morning cell phone calls from the garage were over.

That evening, sitting at the bar, she began to remember in perfect measure how he told her that she was his one true love, the only one who really understood him. *How many bitches did he tell that to?* She took another long pull on the wine and settled in. It was good. The view was perfect.

"Well, hello there," floated the smooth softly southern voice over her shoulder. He ordered a glass of merlot for himself and started talking, about nothing mostly. The dark stranger was grinning from ear to ear. Angel glanced down at his shoes and decided he was worth some conversation. The dental work said he had money and he wasn't wearing a wedding band.

"I'm Howard Clemons."

"Angel Delafuenta. It's nice to meet you," she said, dipping her wrist.

"The pleasure is mine," he said, first kissing her hand, then letting his eyes wander over her bare shoulders. "What brings you to the Ritz?"

"A little vacation."

"What do you do?"

"I'm an accountant by trade," she answered. "I own a boutique firm in Atlanta." The lie had begun. It was the same lie she'd told a dozen times. Men don't want needy women. "Are you here with the conference?"

"I am. I'm on the board of the 100 Black Men," he boasted. "So you could say this is my conference."

"I like a man who knows how to take charge." She managed a grin and took another sip. The conversation went nowhere fast. The handsome stranger was suddenly called away by a colleague and returned only to excuse himself permanently. The second gentleman had recognized Angel from the nightclub and quickly informed his friend. She hadn't heard the conversation, but knew immediately she had been the subject. There were too many familiar faces.

"Men are like parking spots," her mother used to say. "The good ones are taken. The only ones left are marked handicapped."

Deflated, she left the conference early and made the hour-long drive back to Atlanta in complete silence.

Angel's little shotgun bungalow seemed to get smaller every day. The toilet in the only bathroom was clogged and she hadn't taken a shower, let alone washed dishes, in several days. She didn't wake up that morning wanting to die. But all at once, she was tired, lonely, and feeling old beyond her years. She'd gotten out of bed a few times, maybe three or four, but for no longer than five minutes at a time. She shuffled through the dark house, then crawled back under the covers. Watching cars roll by through the slanted blinds, she remembered when she used to dream about things she thought were worth having, worth doing. It was always something. Reliving all that went bad and some of what went good, made no difference to her now.

"Somebody, sometime after I die, will do that," she thought. "They'll gather around the kitchen table at Mama's house and tell funny stories about me. They'll laugh. They'll cry. And then they'll all forget."

The painkillers and the two-liter bottle of water sat on the nightstand waiting. That was the plan. No note. Nothing to explain. Just take the pills and drift off into nothing.

"Angel, are you in there?" a woman's voice called through the mail slot. She heard keys jangling. Stephanie used a spare set to let herself in.

"Girl!" she said as she rushed to the bed. "What happened? What's wrong? I've been calling you. How was the conference?"

"He's gone," Angel replied. She burst into tears.

"Who's gone?" Stephanie asked as she peeled out of her shoes. She climbed into bed next to Angel. Her belly was the size of a basketball.

"Jack. He's gone for good," she sobbed.

"But didn't you meet some eligible bachelors?"

"No. I felt like a pariah. Like I had a big red A on my chest."

"Girl, you look a hot mess. You better get up and move on. It stinks in here."

"I tried calling him, but he won't answer. He won't answer his cell phone and his secretary keeps telling me he's not there."

"Forget about him," Stephanie said with a wave of her hand. "This is about you."

"I can't. I just want to see him."

"He just got back from Chicago."

"How do you know that?"

"Doogie knows him."

"Seth? Why am I not surprised? Atlanta is the biggest small town on earth. I swear everybody I know is somebody's cousin. When were you going to let me in on the big secret?"

"I didn't want to see you hurt. I thought you'd just find somebody new and move on. You always do. You'd be damn fine as hell if you took a bath. A little deodorant wouldn't hurt."

Angel started crying again.

"Doogie works for him."

"Please tell me everything."

"Okay, okay. Damn. Doogie said he went to Chicago right before Christmas chasing after some chick."

Angel let out a deep moan.

"He didn't come back until yesterday. Stayed up there through the holidays. Doogie and the other doctors were scrambling to cover his call schedule. He said something about her granddaddy's funeral in North Carolina."

"What's her damn name?"

"I don't know."

"Yes, you do!"

Stephanie sighed. "Fine. He said her name was Thandy Malone. She's the president of some big investment firm in Chicago. Campbell and . . . Campbell-Perkins. Well, she used to be. I think she quit. Doogie says it's serious and they've been together over ten years. They broke up last July right after you got back from Barbados. He went up there to get her back. That's all I know."

"The hell it is! Tell me everything!" Angel demanded. Her eyes narrowed down to slits.

"Doogie says he's completely caught up with this girl. He even bought her a million-dollar condo."

"He never bought me shit."

Angel slid out of bed and pulled her laptop off the dresser.

"What are you doing?"

"There aren't but so many Thandy Malones in Chicago," she said, sitting on the bed and hoisting the computer onto her lap. "I'm betting just one."

"What good is this going to do? I know I never should have told you that woman's name."

"I'm going to find the bitch." Within a few minutes, Angel had an entire dossier on Thandywaye Mbeki Malone.

"Satisfied?"

"No."

"What in the hell are you going to do with that?" Stephanie pressed, rubbing the fullness of her belly. "Let him go."

"But, I . . ."

"Angel, I said let him go."

Before she hid in her house, she'd driven by Jack's a dozen times. She even rummaged through his mail. Nobody came or went but the maids, and the house was completely dark on Christmas Eve.

"I can't," she admitted. "He promised me."

"He promised you nothing. The man lied. He popped you in the face for heaven's sake. You sat your ass in jail for days until your mother bailed you out. If you don't let go, this will kill you."

"I don't want to die," she said, shaking her head. "I just can't breathe without him."

Stephanie stared blankly at Angel. She noticed the bottle of pills and the waiting container of water.

"Ain't no man worth all of this. Get something for yourself. Something can't nobody take from you." She got up, grabbed the bottle, and took it to the bathroom.

"You got a plunger?"

"Under the sink."

Stephanie worked the clog. When it was clear, she dumped the pills and flushed them away. Angel appeared in the doorway.

"I didn't really want to do it, you know?"

"I know, girl."

"How are you and Doogie doing? Are y'all back together now?"

"Yeah. We're going to the Atlanta Medical Association ball tonight. Doogie's being inducted as president."

"Jack bragged about how he was AMA president a couple of years ago. I know he'll be there tonight. I'm tired of life happening to me." She straightened her back. "My mother always said people make their own luck."

Chapter 28

Along black limousine entered the Gabrielle driveway just after five-thirty, carrying the newly inaugurated governor and his wife. The driver opened the rear door and Faulkner stepped out.

"Hey, Mr. Governor!"

He wrapped his arms around Thandy and planted a kiss on her cheek.

"Stand back and let me look at you!" he said. "Lord, Lord, Lord. You are positively gorgeous!"

"Thank you," Thandy blushed.

"Doc, you know what to do with all of this?"

"Of course, he does," Marla Faulkner said, stepping out of the car. "Thandy, it's so good to see you."

The women hugged politely as the men shook hands. In the beginning, Mrs. Faulkner didn't like the idea that her husband kept company with such a beautiful young woman. Her suspicions almost got the better of her until Sloane agreed to invite Jack and Thandy over for dinner. Besides, Mrs. Faulkner knew well the life of a mistress. She had been Sloane's for several years until his first wife threw him out.

"C'mon in. We can grab a quick cocktail," Jack said.

Jack and Sloane walked ahead. The women trailed behind. Senora Perez opened the double French doors and stood to the side as the foursome walked into the marble foyer. Jack went into the butler's pantry and emerged with a bottle of champagne.

"I think a toast is in order," he said as he popped the cork and poured four glasses. "To Georgia's first black governor."

Everyone raised their glass. The doorbell chimed and Senora Perez opened the front door.

"Y'all drinking without me?" a woman called from the foyer.

"Philly!" Thandy cried out. She turned to Jack. "Sweetie, you didn't."

"Of course I did," Jack said. "She cussed me out first, but she's here."

"Just get me a glass, baby. Everybody meet Frank," Phillipa said, introducing her date. "Frank, this is everybody."

Thandy poured two fresh glasses for Phillipa and Frank.

"Now, let's see. Where were we?" Jack cleared his throat. He raised his glass.

"Careful, doctor. I've got my good eye on you," Phillipa warned.

The cocktail reception was in full swing by the time they arrived. The 191 Atrium filled with tuxedo-clad physicians and their wives. A polite hush took over the room as Jack and Thandy arrived, trailed by the first black governor. The Faulkners faded into the crowd and were soon circled by a gaggle of physicians who wanted to shake his hand. Jack squeezed Thandy's hand and moved into the crowd, stopping frequently to make small talk with his colleagues.

"Don't be nervous, baby," he assured. "This is our night."

"Dr. Gabrielle," a voice came from the fog.

Her smile was unmistakable. Lucy the Lunatic. He forced a grin and said hello.

"It's been a long time."

"Indeed," she said, extending her hand. "I'm Lucy Geautreux. It's a pleasure to finally meet you, Mrs. Gabrielle."

"Good to meet you, Ms. Geautreux," Thandy answered. "It's French, no?"

"Indeed. Creole."

Lucy noticed the empty ring finger and was immediately confused.

"Lucy, meet my friend Thandy Malone."

Lucy frowned, then pasted a smile on her face. "It was good seeing you again," Lucy cooed. "Enjoy the party."

Lucy eased away.

"Who was that?"

"A patient," he lied.

"She's very pretty."

"She is indeed. Let's grab a cocktail. What would you like? Champagne?"

Thandy wondered if she had ever been labeled a patient. She shook the thought away and followed Jack to the bar.

"Dr. Gabrielle!"

"Elijah, my man!"

"And you must be Ms. Malone."

Thandy smiled.

"You're just as beautiful as he told me you were."

"Thank you."

"Thandy, meet my favorite bartender and poker partner, Elijah Brown."

Thandy smiled again and accepted Elijah's best champagne.

The dinner bell sounded. The crowd began to move downstairs to the ballroom, crossing through a palatial hallway that led into the Ritz-Carlton.

"Did I tell you how beautiful you look tonight?"

"Yes, baby. You did."

"And did I tell you how precious you are to me?"

"Yes, baby."

"Did I tell you how much I love you?"

"Only a hundred times today."

"Well, let's make it a hundred and one."

They made their way down the stairs and into the ballroom.

Dressed in a sequined, strapless dress, Angel stepped from the crowd. "Well, hello Jack."

"Angel," he nodded. He wrapped his arm around Thandy and kept going. Angel followed. "Aren't you going to introduce us? Hi, I'm Angel Delafuenta."

Jack tried to pull Thandy away.

"Nice to meet you. I'm Thandy Malone."

"He's a worthless piece of shit," Angel spit out.

"Angel, stop it," Jack demanded.

"What are you going to do? Punch me in the face again?"

Thandy looked at the floor.

"Tell her, Jack. Tell her how you punched me in the face!"

Jack pulled at Thandy's waist, but her feet were firmly planted on the floor. People were staring.

"I don't know who you are or what happened to you," Thandy started. "But, I'm sorry."

Angel lunged. Two men dressed in tuxedos pulled her away. Security was dispatched and she was led from the building.

Against the mumble of the crowd, Jack whispered into Thandy's ear. "I'm sorry, Thandy. I'm so ashamed. I promise I will tell you everything."

"I just want to go home, Jack."

Chapter 29

The fire erupted just before 5:00 a.m. Senora Perez was the first to hit the floor and awake the family. Jack shook Thandy out of a deep sleep and emerged shirtless from the bedroom. The fire alarms blared and the floodlights Etienne had insisted on installing lit up the smoky common areas. Thandy fought her way through the dense smoke to get to the boys. Jack hoisted and carried a drowsy Montana from her bed.

"What's going on?" she cried.

"The house is on fire!" Jack said. "Thandy! Where are you?"

"I've got the boys! Keep going!" she called from down the hallway.

Jack and Montana made it downstairs and into the foyer before the landing gave way. Part of the second floor crashed onto the first.

"Oh my God! Mom! Mom!" Montana screamed.

Jack pushed her out the front door, then dashed up the stairs. He couldn't make the jump across the fiery hole.

"Where's Montana?" Thandy called through the roaring of the fire.

"She's outside! The landing is gone! Go back!" he shouted. "Go back! Take the back stairs."

"I don't know where they are!" Thandy cried, panic in her voice.

"Go back through the boys' room. The study door is on the other side of their bathroom. Get to the stairs!"

Jack thought quickly and ran back down the winding stairwell. He circled through the dining room and into the kitchen. The fire was pouring from everywhere. The boys came out of the back stairs that opened into the keeping room. Thandy had wrapped their faces with wet towels and left every faucet she could get to running at full blast.

"Thandy!"

Jack threw his body against the locked glass door several times. He could see the fear in their eyes. When it wouldn't give way, he wrapped his hand in the curtain and broke the glass. He could hear Thandy and the boys coughing and choking on the thick smoke. Flames shot out of the stairwell. He heard Thandy's screams.

"Baby! Come on!"

He kicked the frame until there was enough room to get through. He pushed his sons through the opening into the arms of a fireman, one at a time.

"Help me," Jack pleaded to the firemen. "Thandy's still inside."

Jack rushed the stairwell ignoring the firemen's orders to come out. The flames blew him back, but he kept going. The firemen rushed the house. The back stairwell fell. Jack fought through the smoky upper hallways searching the rooms, calling her name. He screamed her name again and again, still fighting, still pushing. He kept screaming until nothing came out. He collapsed. He could feel his lungs filling with smoke. *God, Thandy. Please. Get out.*

The streets were clogged with a legion of emergency vehicles, fire trucks, and news crews. Flames shot from the main house, engulfing the nearby cluster of buildings. The curbs were lined with people dressed in their nightclothes, horrified at the site.

Moments later, Thandy stumbled down the driveway, nearly naked and bleeding. A paramedic rushed in and wrapped her in a blanket. The main house collapsed behind them.

"Sweet Jesus!" they heard one woman say. "She's alive."

After two hours, the fire squadron gave up. They set up a safe perimeter and let the structures burn. All that remained were the charred frames. Senora Perez sat curbside next to a paramedic, weeping. The boys were huddled on a neighbor's lawn. Montana lay in the rear of an ambulance, consumed in grief. The children were treated for smoke inhalation at Grady Hospital. Thandy refused treatment until Sloane showed up.

"Let them take care of you," he said. "You sit down there and let that doctor clean out those burns," he ordered.

"Where's Jack?" she whispered.

Sloane was silent.

"Where's Jack?" she pleaded.

He squeezed her hand. "He didn't make it, baby girl."

She cowered over, then dropped to her knees and shrieked. Sloane wrapped his full body around her.

"You said it would get better," she moaned. "You said it was going to be okay."

Chapter 30

Thandy and the children holed up at the Swissotel in Buckhead for the night. The general manager told the family they could stay as long as need be. Little Jack and Jacob were fast asleep on the sofa. Sloane called Yvetta in Winston-Salem.

"Mrs. Malone, I'm so sorry," he told her. "He wanted to love her better."

"He did son," Yvetta said. "I know this. How are they? Where's my grandbaby?"

"She's sleeping now."

"And Thandy? How's my baby?"

"Not good."

Thandy rose from the chair, took the hotel medical kit into the bathroom and began to clean her own burns. She clamped her teeth together and picked the wood and cinder from her forearm. She poured peroxide over the wound and watched it bubble away. Nothing, she thought, could be more painful than losing Jack. Etienne appeared at the door. Thandy could see her in the mirror.

"He's gone," Thandy whispered, bowing her head.

Etienne wrapped her arms around Thandy's head. "I'm sorry," Etienne whispered. "I know how much you meant to him."

Thandy shook her head. She sat on the toilet lid and let out a deep moan.

"Let me see your arm. You need to go back to the hospital. This won't keep."

Thandy nodded again.

"Do you have any money?"

Despite Thandy's silence, Etienne dug into her wallet and pulled out several hundred-dollar bills and the newly acquired American Express Black Card. "Here, take it," Etienne said. "Please, take it."

Thandy looked up at her.

"I understand you saved my, I mean, our sons. I will always be grateful for that."

"You certainly don't owe me anything."

"Please take it."

Thandy finally relented and accepted Etienne's offering.

Etienne went into the main room and picked up the boys, one at a time, and carried them into the adjoining bedroom. Montana woke and reached for them. Etienne placed them under her. Montana wrapped her arms around the boys. Etienne watched them all sleep from a chair by the window.

Sloane sat with Thandy in the main room.

"Your mother will be down here tomorrow noon. I'll send a plane after her. They'll make a stop over in Charlotte and pick up your sister. A car will pick you up and take you over to Peachtree-Dekalb Airport."

"Are you coming?"

"Absolutely."

Thandy nodded.

"There's a detective here to see you. He's downstairs in the lobby."

Thandy got up and put on the new pants and shirt Sloane bought her.

"It ain't much, but it'll get you by."

Sloane called the front desk and invited the detective into the suite.

"Mrs. Gabrielle?"

"Yes, please come in."

Thandy waved her hand across the room.

"Is there some place we can talk in private?"

"It's all right. He's my brother."

"Good evening, Mr. Governor."

The detective took an empty seat. "Mrs. Gabrielle, it's early but our initial investigation tells us this was arson."

"But we had the fireplaces going all day."

"We checked them out. The fire came from several other hot spots. There is evidence of an accelerant in the cellar and on the landing. The carriage house smelled like gasoline. Did anyone other than your family have access to the main house?"

"Just the house staff," Thandy answered.

"How many?"

"Four. Three had gone home for the evening. All have keys. But they wouldn't do this."

"Did you activate your security system?"

"No, I didn't. Jack hadn't given me the code yet. I thought he did."

"Do you know of anyone else?"

Sloane rubbed his arm and asked, "Thandy, is there anybody?"

"Etienne wouldn't do this."

"Who is that, sir?"

"She's Jack's ex-wife. She's in the next room with our children. The divorce was finalized last week."

"I thought you told the officers on the scene that *your* husband died in the fire."

"She was his wife in every way that counts," Sloane explained.

"Look, Etienne got fifteen million," Thandy said. "She wouldn't put the boys in danger."

"I'll have to talk to her. Is there anyone else?" the detective pressed. "Do you know anyone who would want to do you harm?"

Thandy said nothing.

"What about Angel?" Sloane offered. "Angel Delafuenta."

"How do you spell it?"

Sloane spelled it for him. Thandy felt her teeth clamping together.

"She had Jack arrested," Sloane said.

"What were the charges?" the detective asked.

"Assault. They were both charged." Sloane spoke up.

Sloane explained the evening, including the faked pregnancy. He then asked Thandy to get on the phone and call Parham.

"Jack's lawyer can help you understand the issues."

"Where can we find her?"

"She lives in Southwest Atlanta. She called Jack yesterday and at least a hundred times before that," Sloane explained.

"What did she want?"

"She didn't say."

"Did he talk to her?"

"I don't think so. I don't think he ever called her back."

"She was at the gala tonight," Thandy said.

After the investigator left, Sloane promised to tell Thandy everything.

"No," she said shaking her head. "I don't want to know any more."

Chapter 31

Thandy and Montana sat for hours in the grass, saying little, watching the clouds roll across the pastel blue sky. She studied the chiseled marble. She traced his name with her eyes and let the tears fall. Thandy came every Sunday afternoon and never left until the sun went down. She needed to be with him.

It had been almost two years since Jack died. She had spoken at his memorial service, though it had not been expected. She had risen from the front pew, stood in the center of the altar, and said "Courage does not always roar. Sometimes, it is the quiet voice at the end of the day saying, 'I will try again tomorrow.' My name is Thandywaye Mbeki Malone."

She smiled at Etienne.

"He saw past my imperfections and told me I was perfect. He was my friend, when I could not be a friend to even myself. He was my confidante, my constant companion. He was and is the love of my life."

Etienne closed her eyes.

Sloane had been almost too shaken to deliver the eulogy. Montana stood up, walked to the pulpit, and took hold of his hand. He drew his prepared remarks from his suit jacket and put on his glasses. He kissed her face and began. Midway through his remarks, Sloane took off his glasses again to dry his tears and stuffed the paper into his pocket.

"I just want to say what's on my heart. Today isn't only about Dr. Jackson Gabrielle. It's about Thandywaye Malone. Thandy-waye Mbeki Malone is love personified. We witness this in the way she loves her child. In the way she keeps fighting even when the world seems to get the upper hand. We see this in the way she loves us all. It is like witnessing a miracle unfold before our very eyes. But more than anything, I know that she loved her Jack."

Sloane stopped, composed himself, and continued. The sanctuary was silent.

"I am governor today because people like Jack and Thandy Gabrielle believed. When one finds herself faced with darkness," he whispered, "there are but two choices. Let it define and consume you or embrace its meaning and live beyond it. Thandy has spent her entire life living beyond it. Without question, Jack was a better man because of her. He learned how to let somebody love him."

It was almost dark when Thandy and Montana left the cemetery, but they were in no hurry to leave Jack. They slowly made their way back across the green to the road.

"I want to come home," Montana said.

"Why?"

"Yale is too far away."

"You have to finish school."

"I'm transferring to Emory. If it's okay with you, I'd like to stay at home." She gave her mother a strong hug and said, "I want to be with you."

The caretaker watched as they drove away.

Judge Mary Moulton was not sympathetic. After months of sitting in a four-by-four cell awaiting trial, Angel pleaded guilty to one count of arson and one count of manslaughter. To spare the trouble and expense of a trial, the district attorney had agreed to drop four counts of attempted murder in exchange for Angel's plea, but Moulton was not satisfied.

"Miss Delafuenta," the judge said.

Angel stood up with her attorney. She was dressed in a simple blue suit and white blouse. On advice of counsel, her hair was pulled into a tight bun and she wore little makeup. Stephanie, who was sitting several rows back, almost didn't recognize her. Riza sat in the row behind the defendant's table. Thandy, Phillipa, and Sloane sat across the aisle. Etienne sat alone a few rows back. Angel's chin was pressed to her chest.

"Miss Delafuenta, I understand that you have entered into a plea agreement with the D.A.'s office."

"Yes, ma'am."

"I am not inclined to agree. I'm not certain you understand what you've done."

Angel swallowed hard. The defense attorney had warned that the agreement may not stick. There were children in the house. A man was dead, burned until his skin rolled like scarred butter from his bones. Angel had been arrested several days later while having a leisurely lunch with Stephanie. She didn't seem to have a care in the world then.

"You didn't just set a fire. You were so angry, so full of vile, that you broke into a private home and deliberately placed sleeping young children in danger. Do you understand that?"

"Yes, ma'am."

"You also understand that a man in the house died that night and you should be facing first-degree murder while in the commission of a felony?"

"Yes, ma'am."

"Under state law, that would dictate the death penalty. I don't like your deal with the D.A. and it is my sole discretion to honor it. I do not see one reason why you ought to walk the streets a free woman again. I will not honor the agreement before me."

"Your honor, Miss Delafuenta admits to setting the fire," her attorney interrupted. "If you will not honor the plea agreement then I must advise her to go to trial."

"You don't want to test this with a jury, counselor. You do understand that her admission will be entered into evidence?"

The attorney whispered something to Angel, who turned to
look at her mother. Riza nodded her head firmly.

"Your honor, if I can have a moment with my client."

"Court is adjourned until 1:00 p.m." Moulton banged her
gavel. The courtroom emptied.

Riza approached Thandy near the rear doors. "Our family is
very sorry for your loss."

"We appreciate that, ma'am," Thandy answered politely.

"I don't think she wanted anyone to die."

Thandy turned away.

When court reconvened, Angel was sweating.

"Your honor, my client will plead guilty to one count of
felony arson and one count of second-degree murder. She does
not want to put the family through a trial."

The judge sighed. "You do understand what this means, Miss
Delafuenta?"

"Yes, your honor. I do."

"Before I issue a sentence, do you have a statement?"

Angel rose, adjusted her dress, and took out a slip of paper.

"I just want to say that I am sorry. I never meant to hurt anyone. I thought he took everything from me. I was wrong. Because
of what I did, I will lose everything I love. I just want to say that
I am sorry."

"Very well. Will there be any statements from the victims?"

Thandy stood up. "No, your honor."

"Angel Raquel Delafuenta, I hereby sentence you to serve the
remainder of your natural life at the Georgia Correctional Facil-
ity for Women at Hardwick. Further, you will pay restitution to
the victims in accordance with your ability."

Thandy had been satisfied with the sentence.

Epilogue

Thandy sat alone in the den, picking through a stack of mail she hadn't checked in over a week. There was a letter addressed to Montana from her father.

She had been blessed to be loved twice, she thought.

It was January again and the heavens gave her the light blanket of snow she wished for—just in time for baby Jonah's birthday. Learning just weeks after the fire that she was carrying Jack's baby had given Thandy the strength to go on. "*In every blessing there is a curse, a curse in every blessing*," Cump would say.

AUTHOR'S NOTE

I am an insatiable bone collector. I prayed over the "bones" of my own life, the miracles and disappointments alike, the fruits of my personal truths, to give birth to this story. I simply blew the dust off the bones and called them to life. They sprang from the fertile red clay that cakes my imagination like a biblical Lazarus.

I know that somebody somewhere will ask if any of the characters are real, did any of this happen, are you Thandy and if so, then who is Jack (and is he *that* good looking)? Kinda, sorta, in a way, can't tell you, and dear Lord, yes.

I imagine there is some truth in the idea that all good fiction is non-fiction, that all first novels are mostly the autobiographical, therapeutic workings of a troubled mind. My first book, *In My Father's House,* was just about as close to that gristle as I could get without upsetting the marrow. Just as those bones had been set together, I looked around and found a whole 'nuther heap piled up in my closet under my Jimmy Choo shoe boxes. I picked through the fragments like a forensic pathologist, trying desperately to unlock the mysteries of unrequited love.

Indeed, there had been a man, whose very name I once thought divine, who for better or for worse, once upon a time owned my heart—lock, stock, and barrel. I swear the sun didn't rise until he opened up his beautiful brown eyes each morning and placed his perfect toes on the floor. The story of our nearly decade-long love affair would be downright hysterical, if it weren't so painfully tragic. Early on, when I started writing, I used the decayed vestiges of the life we used to have as cartilage and tendons as I began to reset the bones where I thought they should be. And then something almost magical happened. The more I wrote, the more those old bones started doing for themselves.

Even though their spirits reside deep within the "temple of my familiar," the story and the people who inhabit these pages, including Thandywaye and Jackson, are indeed works of fiction. They are what the bones decided to do. I dutifully took dictation. In the end, the fictional Jack Gabrielle didn't want to be the "Jack" that I knew and Thandy Malone didn't find being me so interesting. Although I begged to differ, she won out. They didn't even like our friends and family, so they politely introduced me to theirs.

But truth be told, Thandy and I have many similarities—including, but not limited to, an endless love affair with snow, missing a less-than-perfect father, and a cantankerous grandfather who hated green Jell-O. However, in the interest of full disclosure, my "Jack" would never be caught quoting Shakespeare. Bugs Bunny maybe, but no Shakespeare. It did take him ten years to figure out that he loved me, but by then I was long gone. However, the most important, enduring romance is the one Thandy and I have with ourselves.

Any other similarities to events, circumstances, or persons—living or dead—are unintended and incidental by-products of a bonesetter's work.